Crescent Gold

Crescent Gold

A Novel by

Hal Burton

Novels by Hal Burton

Cave of Secrets

The Penny Red Enigma

Voices from the Mountain

Tubal Cain

cK?m?t kúl

Crescent Gold

Crescent Gold

Crescent Gold

n?[?VƉP \?P ?-- *S'Klallam*

Crescent Gold

Crescent Gold

Although many of the names, places and events are historically true and used to add colorful background, *Crescent Gold* is a work of fiction, and the incidents and characters are products of the author's imagination. Any resemblance to persons living or dead is purely coincidental.

Copyright © 2009 by Hal Burton

All right reserved

Printed and bound by Gorham Printing
    Centralia, Washington

Published by Hal Burton Publishing
    Lilliwaup, Washington

First Edition, First Printing – November 2009

Cover design by Jeanette Burton

Author's photo by Jeanette Burton

Library of Congress Control Number: 2008901245

ISBN – 978-0-9725707-3-2

Crescent Gold

Introduction

Many of my readers encouraged me to write a sequel to my fourth novel, *Tubal Cain*. I must admit I left what happened to several of the main characters somewhat "up in the air."

Did Sven Olsen, the infamous "Warrior", survive the shipwreck of the *S S Valencia*? What happened to Spencer Clayborne and his girlfriend Tressa Monroe after their capture in San Francisco?

Did reporter Jesse Grayson ever write his novel about the murders in the Tubal-Cain mine?

Did Sheriff Jim Albright continue his romance with Sara Munn?

Were more of the gold pendants found?

Leaving these questions unanswered was not for the purpose of setting the stage for a sequel – rather it was my way of ending the story as I did in other novels, letting the reader draw his or her own conclusions.

In retrospect, however, I could see the point that many of you had made, and the more I thought about it, the more I had to agree – *Tubal Cain* needed a sequel. Even I the writer began to speculate about what would have happened to the fictional

Crescent Gold

characters Sven Olsen, Spencer Clayborne and especially, Jim Albright.

Most of the *Tubal Cain* story takes place in Jefferson County, the city of Port Townsend, and at the Tubal-Cain Mine in the Olympic Mountains of Washington State.

Also in Washington State, Lake Crescent and Clallam County are the primary setting for this new tale. However the city of Port Townsend and Jefferson County continue to be central to the story, especially in the early chapters.

The Lake Crescent environs have had a long and colorful history, and much as I did in *Tubal Cain*, I have used real places and events to enhance the background for this novel.

However, the parallel locales and events set in the fifteenth century that involve the S'Klallam people are totally drawn from my imagination.

I would recommend that *Tubal Cain* be read before starting *Crescent Gold* – not an absolute necessity, but it will give one a much broader understanding of the main characters and of the events that occurred before the start of this tale.

A final note – There was a temptation to use actual S'Klallam words in the dialog – a temptation I quickly abandoned. I did, however, use the tribal name and the S'Klallam words for Lake and Gold on a title page.

Crescent Gold

Who They Are

20th Century

Jim Albright – Jefferson County Sheriff

Sven Olsen/Ed Nelson – "Warrior"

Sara Munn – Friend of Jim Albright

Spencer Clayborne – Convicted Smuggler

Tressa Monroe – Girlfriend of Clayborne

Frank Jones – Warrior Gang Member

Jesse Grayson – San Francisco Reporter

Honiko Yamada Grayson – Jesse's wife

Taylor Osgood – Jefferson County Attorney

Rex Thornton – Deep Sea Diver

Ben Maxwell – Clallam County Sheriff

Lily Ellis – Wyle Construction Secretary

Chetzemoka – S'Klallam Tribal Historian

Who They Are

15th Century

Kaiahan – S'Klallam Tribe Member

O'Wota – Mate of Kaiahan

S'Hai-ak – S'Klallam Tribe Member

Prologue

1906

The barnacles cut deep – the pain excruciating, but the alternative was surely a quick death. Ignoring the agony that spread through his body with each hand shift, he moved inexorably toward the lee side of the rock, away from the pounding surf. In between the towering waves he glanced again over his shoulder, and there, faintly visible in the thick froth, was a dark outline. The cliffs of the coastline!

Should he jump and swim toward the image? It could be a mirage or another offshore rock like the one that smashed their lifeboat. Should he chance sapping his remaining strength? The next wave broke his grip, taking the decision out of his hands, first lifting him high, and then with equal force, driving his body under the water.

This was it – he was done, but … *oh*, something was pulling him up. Sven gasped for air.

Crescent Gold

"Got ya!"

At dawn's light the nine men that had reached shore and huddled together during the night awoke to the awesome task that lay ahead. Surrounded by rocks to the north and south, the only way to escape the rising tide was up the 100-foot cliff which loomed behind them. At least they had a chance, for had they been able to see behind the towering rocks, 500 yards to the South, they would have witnessed the passenger steamer *S S Valencia* breaking apart.

A member of the ship's crew, Fred Baker, gathered the men about him.

"Time to get out of here, I'll lead the way." He turned toward Sven, offering his hand. "Baker, Fred Baker, First Mate, I'm the one that pulled you in, last night. You'd better stay close to me; looks like you took quite a beating."

Sven Olsen nodded. "Thanks, ah, name's ... ah, Nelson, Ed Nelson."

An hour later the nine survivors reached the top of the cliff overlooking Cape Beale.

"Look!" shouted Baker, "telephone lines, c'mon."

Following the lines, they came upon a lineman's shack where they found food and a working telephone. It was the result of Baker's call to the nearby Carmanah Light Station on Canada's Vancouver Island that the outside world learned of the shipwreck of the *S S Valencia*.

Baker and the eight others would later find out they were among the 37 survivors, all men. The official death toll would be set at 136 persons, including all the women and children.

Crescent Gold

Part One

Crescent Gold

Lake Crescent

One

1481 A.D.

Dawn was normally her favorite time of the day. The sun had yet to fully rise behind the mountains to the east and its reflected rays on the Great Water had a mystical, yet soothing affect on O'Wota. This daybreak was different.

She'd spent the night alone for the first time since being joined to her mate and today, strangely, eerily, the normally placid water rippled, though there was no wind.

Momentarily ignoring the lake's undulations, she knelt down and blew on the coals, careful to keep the golden pendant her mate had given her away from the growing flames. Kaiahan and the other men should be returning from their summer lodgings before the sun was at its zenith, she thought. They'd be bringing the last of the supplies needed for winter.

As O'Wota rose to get a clay pot, she felt the ground shake – at first gently, next with increased intensity, throwing her to the ground. Then, as if some giant beast had awoken from a long sleep, the earth rose, then fell and the village of Tien-ah slid into the water – deep into the abyss.

Two

1907

Fires destroyed what the earthquake hadn't, but the citizens of San Francisco were a resilient lot, and four months after *Chronicle* reporter Jesse Grayson returned from Washington State, the progress in rebuilding was evident.

Jesse arrived at the *Chronicle* office at seven – too early as far as he was concerned. His wife Honiko had barely enough time to make his lunch before he ran to catch the trolley – one of the few operating. Taking the stairs two at a time, he hurried to his editor's office.

Jay Schilling stood at his second floor window, his back to the open glass-paneled door, not moving, continuing to stare into a gray mist as thick as the smoke cloud hanging over his head. Schilling ran a hand through his silver-gray hair and coughed.

"Fog's lifting. Looks like it'll be a nice day."

Jesse removed his felt pork pie hat, which he wore more often, not so much because of the Bay area's damp, rainy weather, but to cover his fast-receding hairline. He undid the top two buttons of his vest.

Crescent Gold

Not waiting for a reply, Shilling turned and removed the Meerschaum pipe from his mouth and placed it on his desk. "Have a seat, Jesse, and thanks for coming in at this hour. I think you'll understand why I needed to see you early on."

"Sure." He looked for somewhere to put his hat.

"How's that new bride of yours? She's due soon, right?"

"Three months." He fidgeted, twirling his hat; wishing his boss would cut the small talk and get to the point, however he knew from past experience to be patient with Shilling.

"So, you could be gone for a while, say a week or so?"

The fidgeting abruptly stopped. "What?" He had Jesse's rapt attention.

"Here, this came over the wire late yesterday."

Jesse read the UPI story, and reread it, shaking his head all the time. "You want me to cover the trial, don't you?"

"It's your story – who else would I send?" Shilling smiled. "After all, you just might get what you need to finish your book about the murders at Tubal-Cain mine while you're writing the story for the *Chronicle*."

"I'd have to leave tomorrow to get to Port Townsend in time for the trial."

"I know, here." Shilling handed Jesse an envelope. "The ship leaves at noon, Pier 23, your tickets are in the envelope."

Jesse opened the envelope and smiled. "Two sets, round trip, I …"

"Guess I'm a sucker for young love, anyway, I booked rooms at the Carlton Manor. You'd better get a move on; Honiko will need all the time she can to get ready – that is, after she gets over being mad at both of us."

Three

His steel-blue eyes never wavering, Spencer Clayborne paced back and forth, three steps one way, three the other, always careful not to bump the bucket and crockery water container in the corner. Stretching out his arms he'd almost been able to touch the faces of the cement-block walls. The wall above his bunk was partially covered with pictures and news stories from the Port Townsend *Leader*, now illuminated by the light from a small barred window. The only other light came from a twenty watt electric bulb hanging from the ceiling, which was only turned on for two hours at dusk.

He'd been lying on the bunk in the small cell when he got the news from Jefferson County Sheriff Jim Albright. His trial for murder would start in three days. Clayborne surprised himself at how calmly he took the information, but then, he was glad it would finally happen, needed for it to happen. Clayborne's only response to Albright was he wanted to see his lawyer.

Clayborne checked his pocket watch. It had been twenty minutes. *Where was the old man, the no-good son-of-a bitch?*

The court had appointed Taylor Osgood to represent him, but so far other than getting the assault and theft charges

Crescent Gold

reduced, he'd not been worth a plug nickel, but Clayborne wasn't worried. He'd sized up Osgood at their first meeting – seedy, cheap clothes, needing a shave and wearing cologne not quite strong enough to cover up what he guessed was the odor of one too many shots of bourbon at Port Townsend's Black Swan Tavern; he was the perfect choice for Clayborne's escape plan.

He'd never revealed his plan to anyone else except Tressa Monroe, his girlfriend and ex-proprietor of the Crow's Nest, a rest stop on the trail to the Tubal-Cain mine. Her trial for assault and aiding Clayborne in his failed escape to San Francisco had finished last month, and she was now serving time at the women's prison near the city of Forks. Albright said Tressa would be a witness for the prosecution at the murder trial, but Clayborne knew otherwise.

Damn! Where is Osgood? He was sure the old reprobate would fall in line. Clayborne knew greed was always the big motivator for the corrupt attorney. The clanging of the cellblock door and approaching footsteps stopped his pacing.

"It's about time!"

"What's the rush, Clayborne?" Albright said, as he opened the door to the cell and ushered in Taylor Osgood. "You're not going anywhere, soon." The sheriff smiled. "Oh, I forgot, maybe to the gas chamber."

Clayborne ignored the sarcasm and with a flourish, motioned for Osgood to sit on the bunk. Then he swirled quickly, glaring at Albright through his scraggy black hair. "Don't be too sure – now if you'll get lost, me and my fine attorney here have lots to talk about. He hesitated, sat down

Crescent Gold

and put his arm around Osgood. "Say, how 'bout being a good host for my legal-eagle here, I'm sure he'd like a good cup of coffee and so would I."

"Always the smart ass aren't you Spencer. Sure, why not, part of the County's service for a leading citizen like yourself. I'll have Larry bring you some."

"Whoa, there, ole Deputy Larry is back on days? No, no, he still has it in for me and Tressa – probably poison the coffee. Wasn't me that clobbered him," Clayborne laughed loudly and slapped his knee. "Just kidding, big Jim. Bye the bye, you can have Larry empty the honey-bucket while he's at it," pointing to the corner. Clayborne pinched his nose. "Phew!"

Albright slammed the cell door shut. "Do you want the coffee, or not?"

Clayborne set the empty coffee mug aside. "Okay, so you understand, I need you to do exactly as I've said. No slip ups." He squeezed Osgood's thigh, making the attorney wince. "Now, I've written down some other things you'll need. Here." He reached under his bunk mattress and removed several sheets of paper, handing them to Osgood. "We've only got two days."

"I don't see any map." Osgood awkwardly set his cup down, sloshing coffee on his nicotine-stained fingers and on the floor. He slid nearer the end of the bunk.

"Don't worry about that. In good time my man, in good time. Now, let's go over the details before that asshole Sheriff returns."

Crescent Gold

Albright put a finger to his lips as his deputy walked by, and getting the message, Larry closed the door with a bang and exited the cell block.

Attorney/Client privilege aside, the sheriff strained to hear what Clayborne was saying, but from his hiding place in the corner, all he heard was an occasional word. If he moved any closer he'd be seen.

The long investigation of the Tubal-Cain murders, the battles with Clayborne and Menucci, his wounds, and his failed attempt to capture Sven Olsen had taken their toll on Jim Albright. Just that morning he'd noticed several gray hairs creeping into his flaxen hair, a few extra crow's feet, and Sara Munn had commented more than once that his hazel eyes had lost a bit of their sparkle.

His two deputies, Larry and Stan had reminded him the other day that Brinnon's native son and Port Townsend's most eligible bachelor would soon be turning thirty.

Ugh.

What was that! Osgood was calling for Larry. He pushed back into the corner.

Crescent Gold

Four

The *Vancouver World* had the story on the third page of the second section, and Sven Olsen almost missed it. He was mesmerized and didn't hear his name being called for the second time.

"Ed, Ed Nelson, c'mon time to get back to work." His foreman didn't yell again, but closed his lunch box and headed for the construction site.

The structure was to be the tallest office building in Vancouver, British Columbia, and was scheduled to be ready for occupancy in four months. It would be the second office building opened in 1907. Sven had been on the crew for two months and although initially he had planned to leave Canada as soon as possible after the *Valencia* incident, he'd decided some time getting accustomed to his new persona was a good idea, and after reading the ad for experienced construction workers, hired on at Larson Construction Ltd.

The story of Spencer Clayborne's impending trial in Port Townsend rated only one column, but the story had stuck in his craw all day, so by quitting time, he'd made up his mind. He would go to the trial. *Am I that stupid? Why?* He'd safely snuck away from the mine in Copper City last year, recovered

Crescent Gold

most of his hidden cache of money and survived the *Valencia* shipwreck. The old adage about curiosity and the cat came to mind. Still, *no one will recognize me.*

Gone was the beard and mustache, gone was at least thirty pounds, and gone was the sandy hair, now colored a dark auburn. He looked ten years younger, and when he wore his new horned-rimmed glasses, he looked nothing like Sven Olsen, the former general foreman of the Tubal-Cain Copper Mine, leader of a gold ore smuggling ring, accomplice to two murders, the killer of brothel manager Ella Brown, and the man his gang had called "Warrior". His only flub was an occasional fall back to Swedish brogue or a sporadic Swedish swear word when he got frustrated over some difficult task. He'd been diligently practicing the inflections of a Canadian accent, even to the point of saying "zed" rather than "z".

It was the last two lines in the *World* article that convinced him he had to go, foolhardy or not.

The article said that hidden in the dress of Clayborne's female disguise when he was apprehended were seven gold pendants, his girl friend Tressa Monroe had one hanging around her neck, and six more were found in his luggage. *That lying cheat*, Sven thought; all that time Clayborne, and likely his buddy Vince Menucci, had been keeping the pendants secret. *Were there more where those had come from? Were all of them from the cave where they'd found the gold ore? They must be worth a small fortune.*

The temptation was too strong and revenge clouded his judgement – he'd leave tomorrow.

Five

Spencer Clayborne had spent many hours studying the drawings on the wall of the cave above the tunnel at the Tubal-Cain copper mine – the wall that had become a pile of rock after the earthquake, the quake he'd barely survived. At first he believed they were typical Indian drawings, symbolizing fertility or chronicling whaling, like the petroglyphs he'd seen etched on rocks near Lake Ozette and Cape Alava.

His assumptions changed when he visited the library in Port Townsend. Buried in the depths of the library he found a book describing ancient wall paintings of the early inhabitants of the Olympic Peninsula, especially the S'Klallam nation, and the more he researched, the more he became convinced the drawing on one section of the cave wall was a map. The shape of the elevated hump on the far right resembled Iron Mountain, the very mountain where the cave was. On his third visit, he stole the book, frustrated that he had been only able to go to the library on his infrequent trips. Clayborne had been certain, that given time, he'd be able to decipher the symbols and solve the puzzle of mysterious drawings.

Crescent Gold

Eventually he became convinced that the illustration shown at the left edge was that of a lake, because it showed a heron standing in a circle. The heron was one of the S'Klallam symbols for water. Even though the circle showed ripples, which probably indicated waves, the water was entirely surrounded by land. The same depiction of the heron was on one side of all the gold pendants he'd found in the cave. Just above the crescent-shaped body of water, in all the pictures, loomed what Clayborne thought must be another mountain, and towering over the mountain was the figure of a man hurling what looked like long pointed sticks.

Clayborne had secreted the book in a niche in the cave. He'd been tempted to discuss his research with his partner Vince Menucci, but decided he'd best keep his thoughts to himself and Tressa Monroe. The earthquake had buried the book and several pendants hidden with it.

His drawings of the cave wall depictions, however, had been safely hidden with a friend in Irondale before his flight to San Francisco. Clayborne's plan had always been to return to Washington someday, unravel the mysterious symbols and if he could discover the precise location at the west end of the trail – something told him there was a treasure to be found; a treasure very likely involving gold pendants.

As Jim Albright reached the top of the hill and turned onto Jefferson Street, he stretched his six-foot frame and looked up at the clock on the courthouse tower. He knew he would be late, because the tower bell had rung ten minutes ago. Reaching the entrance, he took the steps to the judge's offices

Crescent Gold

two at a time and with a sense of renewed exhilaration, knowing the long awaited trial of Spencer Clayborne would start in three days. It would be none too soon. Judge Fleming said it should be a quick trial, and he hoped so, as he'd put his budding romance on hold, and Clayborne was long overdue for his just desserts.

He'd only been able to see Sara Munn four times since leaving her in Copper City, when he'd chased after Sven Olsen, whom he had identified as the leader of the gold ore smuggling ring, the man his gang had called, "Warrior".

The first time he saw her was when he returned to Copper City to bring Frank Jones to the jail in Port Townsend. His capture of Jones had ultimately led to the solving of the two murders at the Tubal-Cain Mine, and the breakup of Sven Olsen's gang. Sara Munn was still in Copper City nursing the last of the patients that had been injured in the earthquake, but Jones was not. Albright knew that not having the miner as a witness at Clayborne's trial might hurt their case; especially since all the other gang members were presumed dead. His own testimony, trail boss Sarge Hornsby's and Tressa Monroe's would have to suffice. He had Jesse Grayson's statement, but the possibility of the *Chronicle* reporter attending was remote.

Frank Jones had overpowered the mineworker left to guard him in the powerhouse and disappeared the night before the sheriff returned. Albright vented his disappointment at mine Superintendent Bishop, had dinner at the cookhouse with Sara and returned alone to Port Townsend the next day.

Crescent Gold

Since then, Albright had traveled twice to see Sara at the family turkey farm in Chimicum, and then just last week, she'd come to Port Townsend. He knew that meeting only four times in the last six months was not a successful recipe for continuing a romance. He imagined the vivacious Miss Munn likely had entertained several suitors.

He needn't have worried, for as it turned out, the two nights in Port Townsend made up for lost time.

Six

Arnold Fleming's courthouse office décor matched his dress and demeanor – Draconian in every aspect. In fact, calling Judge Fleming's behavior severe and unsympathetic didn't do him justice. Albright couldn't have been more pleased. Clayborne was sure to get the harshest sentence, which in this case was death, if they could prove he was an accomplice to both the murders at the mine.

Fleming was seated behind his small wooden desk, barren of everything, save a single inkwell and several sheets of paper. He laid down the pen as Albright was shown in.

"You are late Sheriff, close the door."

"Yes, I know," said Albright, forgoing any excuse, no matter how reasonable.

"All right, let's talk about this case for a few minutes, before Osgood and Lasley get here."

"Isn't that a no-no?" Albright ventured, risking the judges wrath. "Nate Lasley is going to be just as mad as that old coot Osgood if he finds out you and I discussed things without him."

Crescent Gold

"I don't give a you-know-what about that. Nate's going to prosecute this for all it's worth and the reason I assigned the "old coot" as you call him, to be Clayborne's attorney, was so there'd be no doubt about the outcome. So, don't go queasy on me, I'll worry about the propriety of our conversation. Now, what's the story on your witness Tressa Monroe? Without that Frank Jones character, you need her as a witness."

"I know. My new deputy Stan is already on the way to get her."

"What about the trail boss, Rueben Hornsby? I hear tell he's a loose cannon – a bit unreliable."

"The train from Quilcene was late, but Sarge is here and checked into his room at the hotel. As far as reliability, Sarge has always been dependable."

"Good. Now on another subject, I got this wire an hour ago." He handed the telegram to Albright.

"So, Jesse Grayson will be here. Great! It'll be good to see him again. I imagine they'll be plenty of other reporters, too. Some gent from the *Seattle P I* was checking in when I was at Sarge's hotel."

"Just be sure we don't end up like some carnival side show. If I have to, I'll kick out all the newspaper people. Lasley would like nothing more than to have this be a big circus with him as the ringleader. You take care of that."

There was a knock on the door. "That will be our two lawyer friends, why don't you let them in."

Crescent Gold

Seven

1481

Kaiahan was only a mile from the village when the earthquake began. He and the other men were thrown to the ground, but managed to escape with minor injuries. They gathered their supplies and raced to Tien-ah, hoping for the best, but fearful of what they'd find.

Their fears were justified.

Where once had been their winter home of Tien-ah, there was only water. The earth where cedar lodges and the longhouse once stood was gone except for a few rocks at the edge of the lake. Huddled near the rocks on what had become a narrow point of land, were the survivors, among them, Kaiahan's mate, O'Wota.

He ran to her, as did the other men who were lucky enough to find members of their families alive, happy that the great Storm God that lived above the mountain had spared them.

Crescent Gold

In all, only thirty-one members of the tribe set out that night, returning to their summer home on the Iron Mountain, apprehensive of the arduous trip, the grueling climb to their caves, and the winter ahead.

Kaiahan was chosen to lead the way. At age twenty-four he was one of the older tribal members and O'Wota had little trouble concealing her pride at walking beside her mate.

The knee-length tunic of woven cedar bark did little to conceal his tanned, sinewy body. Shoulder length black hair and a full mustache added to Kaiahan's aura of virility.

Eight

The loud knock at his apartment door startled Taylor Osgood awake. He'd been expecting the two men, but after one too many shots of Old Forester, he'd passed out. He picked himself up off the floor. "Yes, just a minute."

Osgood had earlier met the man who called himself Jake at The Brown Lantern Tavern. Unlike "Jake" who was tall, near Osgood's age of fifty, thin as a rail and neatly dressed, the other was young, unkempt, considerably overweight, and with several days' growth of beard, barely covering his pockmarked face.

Jake brushed by Osgood and, barely allowing time for his partner to enter, closed the door. "Looks like you started without us." He picked up the half empty bottle of bourbon off the floor and walked to the small kitchen counter, grabbing an empty glass. "Want a shot?" he said to his cohort, who by now had plopped on the couch.

"Sure, but make it a double, it was a long ride."

Jake filled two glasses and turned toward the lawyer, whose bulbous nose was beet red. "Want another, Osgood? Oh,

Crescent Gold

oh, looks like there's not enough," he said, as he downed one glass and refilled it. "Okay, let's get down to business."

"Yea, business," said the short man, "like four hundred bucks is not enough."

"That's all I can offer," Osgood replied, regaining his composure. "I already told Jake that Clayborne can only lay his hands on that much."

Jake glared at his partner. "Shut up! We'll worry about that later. C'mon Osgood, let's go over the plan again so we're all on the same page."

During the next fifteen minutes, Osgood reviewed Clayborne's scheme, the one he'd been talked into abetting, and if successful, the one which would make him rich beyond his wildest imaginings. He'd heard rumors about a secret cache of gold near Lake Crescent, but like most, had scoffed at the tale. Clayborne's story, the evidence of the gold pendants, and his belief that his client really did have a map to the location, convinced Osgood beyond any doubt that there was a treasure waiting to be found. As far as he was concerned, Jake and his runt of a partner would do their part and be none the wiser. Only he would share the prize with Clayborne.

"So, questions, anybody?" Osgood asked.

"No, I think it's pretty clear. Just one thing, though, you'd better not screw up as far as the horses are concerned."

Nine

Sailing out of San Francisco on the *Wawona* had been a pleasant surprise, and tranquil seas a welcomed blessing. Jesse needn't have worried about how Honiko would do on the voyage to Port Townsend, she was fine. It was he, even with calm summer-like weather so late in the year, who had twice frequented the side of the ship. Honiko was especially pleased to reacquaint herself with Captain Jacobs, the man who had married them on their previous passage.

It was Jacobs, now seated across from them in the ship's dining room, who was smiling broadly and chuckling so loudly that the other passengers were staring at their table.

"So, little Miss Honiko, not so little anymore." Jacobs laughed at his joke. "I can't believe the doctors allowed you to travel, but then from what I've heard, you are doing fine. Not like some people," he said, looking at Jesse, and laughing again, only louder.

"Wasn't that long ago that I had that devil Clayborne on my ship, first trip dressed as a woman, and then in shackles when we delivered him to Sheriff Albright. Seems just like yesterday." The captain rose and offered his hand to Jesse. "Thanks for the conversation. I need to check with the bridge.

Crescent Gold

And Grayson, good luck with the trial and your story, and take good care of this lady of yours." He nodded at Honiko. "We dock at one, so have a good night's rest." He paused. "It might be a bit choppy when we pass Cape Flattery and enter the Strait, so it might be a good idea to eat breakfast early."

Honiko waved excitedly, her pageboy-cut black hair bouncing up and down. "Look! There is Sheriff Albright."

Jesse had wired the sheriff and was pleased to see him standing at the gangway. They'd been through a lot together since that first pack-mule train ride from Quilcene to Copper City. It didn't seem so long ago that they'd seen the bodies of the two slain miners, survived the ambush by Spencer Clayborne, lived to tell of their almost deadly encounter with Clayborne's partner Vince Menucci, survived the earthquake, and rescued Honiko from those who would have forced her into a life of prostitution.

To Jesse, Jim Albright looked much the same, and although almost thirty, he still had a youthful appearance that deluded some to underestimate his resolve and professionalism. Many a Jefferson County maiden's daydreams were filled with thoughts of conquest of the tall bachelor sheriff with the lanky frame, wavy hair and welcoming smile.

The sheriff returned Honiko's wave, and yelled to Jesse. "I've got a carriage. Meet you in the passenger terminal."

As they walked to the gangway, Honiko turned to Jesse. "I wonder if the sheriff is still, ah … how do you say, 'seeing' Miss Munn."

Crescent Gold

"I think so. Last time we talked, he said she was back at her parent's turkey farm. She's probably busy with Thanksgiving Day next month."

Honiko smiled. "You will have to explain again to me about your Thanksgiving Day celebration. It sounds much like my country's *Kinro kansha no hi*, the annual thanksgiving for the harvest."

"Do they eat turkey?" Jesse smiled and took her hand.

"No, rice. It is when our Emperor dedicates the year's rice harvest to the spirits, and tastes the rice for the first time." She smiled back and gently squeezed his hand. "But I am American, now, so I must learn of your … our celebration."

Crescent Gold

Ten

The crossing from Victoria to Port Townsend took only forty minutes and Ed Nelson used the time to go over his travel documents. He'd lost his credentials when the *Valencia* sunk, but that turned out to be a piece of good fortune, for he had been able to establish his Canadian identity without any detailed investigation. Fortunately ten of the United States bank notes he'd gotten before embarking on the *Valencia* had been safely secreted in the lining of the coat he wore in the lifeboat, so there had been sufficient funds to cover the documentation costs and provide for a small apartment in the city.

The single-sheet certificate contained a description of Citizen Edward Nelson and was embossed with the official seal of the Canadian government. He would have no difficulty entering the United States.

Ed walked down the ramp to the terminal, confident, but ever mindful of the possibility that someone could recognize him as Sven Olsen. His constant thought – *I'm crazy to do this.*

Crescent Gold

The desk clerk rotated the register with a flourish, scanning down to the newest entry. "Welcome to The Palace Hotel, Mr. Nelson. Here's your key, room 103, our very best."

Ed took the key without saying anything and turned to leave.

"First time in Port Townsend?"

"Ah … yes, first time," Ed said, almost answering no.

"Lots of excitement in town tonight and tomorrow, you picked a good time to visit."

Ed nodded and reluctantly paused as the gregarious clerk seemed hell bent on telling him all the local news whether he wanted to know or not.

"Tonight's the opening of the Rose Theater. Just around the corner on Water Street. A brand new play, by Ross Bennett. They may have a few seats left." He continued on. "Then on Wednesday, the trial of Spencer Clayborne begins – should be a lu lu, lots of people in town for that one."

Nelson's ears perked up at mention of the trial, but his expression showed no interest. "Sounds interesting, but I'm here on business, and now, if you'll excuse me …."

"Sure, sure. Let me know if you need anything Mr. Nelson, name's Henry, Henry Farris."

"There is one thing, I'm hungry. Where's a good place close to get a meal?"

"The Black Swan Tavern serves till two o'clock, just around the corner – two blocks."

Eleven

Taylor Osgood's favorite noontime meal was Sheppard's Pie, and today was no exception as he sat alone at one of the small tables at the Black Swan. He always followed the mashed potato topped casserole with one stiff drink to get him through the day. Today, however, the day before the trial, he had continued ordering refills when he should have been back in his office polishing up his opening statement. As drink five was being poured, a man he had earlier noticed sitting at the bar walked to his table.

"May I join you?" he asked, and sat down before Osgood could respond.

Osgood hunched he shoulders. "Looks like you already have … ah … sure, I …" He slurred his words.

"Thanks. I'm new in town, here on business. Barman there says you're up to snuff on most everything here 'bouts."

Osgood threw out his chest. "He's got that right, lived here most of my life. Bet your life, ah, what ya say your name was?"

"Didn't, name's Nelson, Ed Nelson, and you are Mr. Osgood, the towns leading attorney, I understand."

"Call me Taylor," he said smiling, and downed half the glass of Jack Daniels.

"I had trouble finding a room. Seems everyone's in town for the trial ... here, let me get us a couple more drinks." He waved at the bartender and made a 'V' sign with his fingers. "Two more of the same!"

"Everyone seems to be talking about this fellow, ah ... what's his name, Clayson," Nelson continued.

"It's Clayborne, and he's my client," Osgood said, again puffing up his chest like a male peacock as the bartender brought the drinks. "Good ole Spencer Clayborne. One sneaky bastard, too, peopl' see ... ah, the sons a bi ...?"

Nelson said nothing, but sipped at his drink. Osgood rambled on.

"Yeah, he's something else, but no fool, always got an ace in the hole." Osgood raised his glass. "Thanks. Now I'd better get going ... big stakes, here ... should get me out of this fleabag of a town."

"Getting a big fee for this one, huh?" Nelson asked.

"Nah, stinking peanuts, Court appointed me, but as they say, 'there's gold in them thar hills'." He laughed and rose to leave. "All you have to do is know the w ... ah, oops, time to go." He staggered toward the door and Nelson got up to steady him.

"Here, let me help."

Twelve

Jim Albright eased out of the lobby chair as Jesse approached. "How's the room?"

"Great and I'm starved, and I would love to get brought up to date. I'll even buy!"

"Ah, the famous reporter is flush with coin." He hesitated. "Where's Honiko?"

"Resting, it was a long voyage, but she's really got sea legs, unlike yours truly."

Albright smiled. "Still get queasy at sea, huh?"

"Yes, unfortunately I still do." He nodded. "But right now I could eat a cow. As I recall, the Black Swan is just down the street?"

"What about your wife, isn't she hungry, too?"

"I had some tea and biscuits sent to the room. That's all she wanted. Let's go."

Albright jumped out of the way of the first man, but Jesse wasn't quick enough to avoid the stout, gray-haired man who swung through the doors.

Crescent Gold

"Son n' bitch, watch out where you're goin," the older man glared at Albright, shouted at Jesse, and not stopping, walked away from them, following the auburn haired younger man.

Albright watched them move away. "You okay, Jesse?"

"Yeah. Do you know that old fart? He looked as drunk as a skunk."

"That was Taylor Osgood. Local town joke, but he's a lawyer, and what a coincidence, he's Clayborne's."

"No kidding. That is a twist of fate. Who's the other one?"

"Didn't get a good look at him, but don't believe I know him? Something about that walk, though – mm, no, don't think so."

The Black Swan was nearly deserted, the gas lights either side of the ornate mirror behind the bar were now turned on full as evening approached. They'd been talking for over two hours, and Jesse had a dozen pages of notes. The two friends had spent several minutes eating and reliving their adventures of the previous year: the first time they'd gone into the Tubal-Cain mine, the investigation of the two deaths, sneaking Honiko away from Copper City, Clayborne's ambush on the way to Quilcene, the earthquake that nearly killed them, and Jesse and Sarge Hornsby's capture of Clayborne.

"Just think, Jim, it was right here at the Black Swan where I cracked that chair leg on Clayborne's noggin." Jesse had said.

Now, over an hour later, Jesse laid down his pencil and stretched his arms. "So you think there's no way he's going to get off?"

Crescent Gold

"Nope. I do feel a bit guilty with Judge Fleming appointing Osgood as Clayborne's lawyer. Bastard should get a fair trial, but I'm sure Fleming picked him just to make sure there'd be a conviction. With that shark Lasley as the prosecutor, though, I don't think anyone would do any better, so, maybe its poetic justice that Clayborne who once had all that booty, can't afford a decent attorney."

The clock on the wall to the right of the mirror chimed three times. Jesse checked his pocketwatch. "Wow, it's late. Honiko's probably wondering where I am. Listen, Jim, thanks, I'd better get going. Are you doing anything later tonight?"

"I'm catching the three-forty train to Chimicum to see Sara, and then back here in the morning. Jury selection starts at ten."

Jesse offered his hand. "Better let you go then. Thanks. I'll see you at the courthouse, and if you do need another witness, I'm ready."

Thirteen

The town of Chimicum was the first stop of two on the route from Port Townsend to Quilcene. During the week, only one passenger car was used, the balance were freight cars, primarily loaded with equipment and supplies for the Tubal-Cain Mine. The Quilcene station was next to Worthington's Store, where the loads destined for the mine were off-loaded and staged for pick-up by Sarge Hornsby's pack-mule train. Sara's parent's farm was two miles from the Chimicum station and Albright had telephoned ahead so Sara could meet him with her buggy.

Albright never ceased being awed by Sara's radiant green eyes and glistening auburn hair that always smelled like freshly picked lavender. This afternoon, the hair was not pulled back and held with a bow, but atypically hung loose, gently stirring in a late afternoon breeze. He tapped his pipe on his shoe heel, picked up his small overnight bag, and waved to her as the train slowed.

Crescent Gold

The conductor yelled, "Chimicum, Chimicum, next stop Leland. Train leaves in five minutes."

"You look beautiful, as usual, Miss Munn," Albright said, as he swung down from the still moving train, dropped his bag and took her in his arms.

"Why thank you Mr. Sheriff." She smiled broadly, stretched up and kissed him on his cheek. "How was the trip?"

"Short and uneventful – not like the mess I left behind. I'll hate going back tomorrow."

"I don't like you leaving, either. C'mon, buggy's tied behind the station, suppers going to be late as it is."

"Your mom fixing us a big meal?"

"No, I am. Mom and Dad are at my grandparents place over in Leland. So I don't want to hear any complaints."

"You mean we're alone tonight?" He helped her into the buggy.

She smiled. "Looks that way. Hope you don't mind?"

Albright untied the horse and climbed into the seat next to Sara. "Ah … well … I don't know what to say, I …"

Sara put a hand over his mouth. "Just hush and say 'giddy up'."

He couldn't hold back the burp. "Sorry about that. I've read in some countries burping is a sign of appreciation for a good meal." Albright smiled.

"I don't know, but glad you liked it." She giggled and reached across for his empty plate. "Let's have dessert later."

"I'll help with the washing," he said quickly. Jim picked up the remaining dishware and followed Sara into the kitchen.

Crescent Gold

"That would be nice." She reached the sink and turned back toward him. "You know, people are talking about us, especially after my trip to Port Townsend."

He set down the dishes and moved next to her. "You stayed with the Fletchers and I always left by eight. Besides, if they talked about us after that, think about what they'd say if they knew your folks were gone tonight."

They decided it would be practical if he did the washing and she dried and put things away as she would know where things went. She was hanging a damp towel over a rack when Jim came up behind her. Tensing at first, Sara relaxed as his arms encircled her waist, pulling her to him. She shivered as he kissed the nape of her neck and then nibbled on her earlobe.

"If they're talking about us anyway, we've got nothing to lose, have we?"

She softly uttered his name. "Jim …we've …"

"We've what, said we'd wait?" His hands slowly moved upward from her waist and over her breasts. He took her silence as consent and began stroking her nipples.

She knew that now was the time to move if she was going to pry herself away, but instead she found herself pushing back against his firmness, welcoming the heat of his hands as they began to wander over the rest of her body.

"I guess the apple pie can wait," she said, turning in his arms and raising her lips to meet his. He pulled away.

"Hm? Don't know, apple pie, you say, well …" He lowered his head and sought her welcoming lips.

Fourteen

The sun was slowly dropping behind Port Townsend's courthouse clock tower and two blocks away, Ed Nelson turned up the gaslight flame on the bedroom wall in Taylor Osgood's small apartment and returned to the upholstered rocking chair. Osgood had been out cold for an hour.

Nelson had carefully searched the Cheval dresser, the walnut writing desk and the night stand. The only thing untouched was the commode chair. If the lawyer had anything relating to Clayborne, it wasn't at his residence. Osgood had cried out to someone named Jake and rambled on about some map, but he couldn't make sense out of it. Nelson was double checking under the bed when Osgood had coughed.

"What the hell … oh damn … how long have I been out?"

"Maybe 'bout an hour. Had quite a time getting you here."

"Oh shit … Nelson, isn't it?" Osgood glanced at the Ingraham mantle clock by his bed, its green swirl marbleized pillars and decorative brass face the only remotely ornate thing in the room.

"Yeah, Ed Nelson, from Canada, remember?"

"Listen, I owe you one, but now, I need to get to my office. I really appreciate you getting me here. God, it's after six." He

Crescent Gold

hesitated. "Didn't blather on too much, did I? Tend to talk a lot when I'm, well, you know, sleeping it off."

"No, no, glad to help. You did mention a map several times, and someone named Jake ... must be important. I figured it had something to do with your trial, huh?"

Osgood's ruddy complexion turned a pale white, and his intake of air was very audible. "Ah ... no ... must have been thinking about a ... a trip I'm going to take."

Nelson thought to himself. *You lying old windbag. I'll bet it damn well has something to do with the trial and Clayborne. Who's this Jake character?*

"Oh, well anyway, glad you're feeling better. Guess I'd better get going. Almost time for supper." Nelson rose and walked to the door. "Good luck tomorrow, nice meeting you."

Instead of going to The Palace Hotel for his meal, Nelson waited in the shadows and followed Osgood as he made his way, staggering down Jefferson Street. He'd expected him to go to his office, but instead the lawyer continued on, and several blocks later entered the Brown Lantern Tavern.

The upper half of the Brown Lantern's windows were not curtained, so Nelson was able to watch as Osgood wove his way to the rear of the tavern and slid into a booth. It looked as if two men faced Osgood, but he could only clearly see one, who appeared to be short, looked unshaven, and probably in his early twenties. Only the shoulder and arm of the other was visible.

Now what do I do? Nelson thought.

Fifteen

On the third day the tribe reached the trail to the caves. All but one of their small band had survived the rugged trek, and they'd buried the old man under a pile of rocks near the source of the river they called "Elwha".

Kaiahan estimated the freezing level to be several thousand feet above them, so he and the other men reasoned their ascent would be uncomplicated by snow or ice. Hopefully, they would reach the entrance to the main cave by nightfall.

The largest cave served as the tribe's gathering place and was connected to four smaller family caves by a series of tunnels. This had been their summer home for ages. How it would serve them now would depend on many things, the least of which would be available food and water – a severe winter could doom them. The men had argued over the merits of returning to the mountain or rebuilding the village on the lake. Kaiahan had advocated returning. And he had prevailed.

Crescent Gold

The tribe reached the cave at dusk.

Besides serving as their gathering place, the large grotto was used for many purposes. All tribal ceremonies were held here, the tribe often cooked together after a hunt and most important, because of the metal ore found by their ancestors, it was where they fashioned the pendants used for trade in the summer, at potlatches, and for special recognitions.

The process of extracting the ore, "smelting" it and forming it into the beautiful pendants had been passed down from generation to generation. Tribal legend had it that an ancestor who once lived by the Great Sea to the west brought the secret with him from a faraway land. They called the smelting method, "Ming-na ta" after their ancient forefather.

Kaiahan was not a skilled metal craftsman; however he, like his father and grandfather before him, was the tribe's historian, the one who chronicled the important events in their lives. Using symbols learned under his father's tutelage, he recorded on the cave's walls the significant happenings of each year.

On the third day after their arrival, Kaiahan began the painstaking job that would take him weeks to complete. All had agreed the most important wall depictions should be the illustrated story of the village's destruction and their just-completed journey.

There was universal fear that for whatever reason, the great Storm God had punished them and he may not allow a return for many years. Future generations would need the location of

Crescent Gold

the old village. Perhaps they'd be able to recover the hundreds of pendants that had sunk with their winter home.

Sixteen

The train had pulled into the station on schedule, and Jim Albright was hurrying to the jail. It had been quite a night, one filled with heated passions, sensations he'd never known, and promises of a future life together. He couldn't wait for the trial to be over.

"How's our prisoner?" he asked Larry, entering the office.

"Seems fit as a fiddle; his usual smart-ass self."

"Okay, as soon as he's done eating, get him ready to go. I've got to get over there now, so see you … ah … in fifteen minutes. Don't be late or Judge Fleming will blow a gasket."

Judge Arnold Fleming swung the gavel down so hard, the Lady Justice statue on the corner of his high bench toppled off, nearly hitting the clerk on the head.

Jesse had trouble not snickering, but several people near him did.

"Come to order!" Fleming shouted, his face reddening, his jowls bouncing, and his tone daring anyone in the packed courtroom to defy him. Again, "Order!"

"Mr. Lasley, Mr. Osgood, we will begin jury selection."

Taylor Osgood nodded at the judge and rose from his seat next to Spencer Clayborne.

It was Clayborne's earlier entrance that had thrown the courtroom into a frenzy. Shackled and escorted by Deputy Larry and Sheriff Albright, he nevertheless smiled broadly, waved at everyone, in particular at Judge Fleming and at the top of his lungs, shouted obscenities to the prosecuting attorney, Nate Lasley.

Two hours and six challenges later, a jury of twelve of Port Townsend's male citizenry were seated for the trial. Clayborne had been quiet throughout the process in sharp contrast to his earlier behavior. Only once did he talk to Osgood.

Judge Fleming swore in the jury and thanked them for their willingness to serve. With that, he rose and struck his gavel.

"We will hear opening arguments at nine sharp tomorrow morning."

"Your honor," Osgood raised his arm, "I'd like a few minutes in private with my client before he returns to his cell."

"Very well, you can use the bailiff's office. The sheriff can take you there."

Albright pulled Clayborne to his feet and moved toward the rear of the courtroom. "C'mon Osgood, and Clayborne, no funny business, I'll be right outside the door and Larry will be outside by the window."

Crescent Gold

"Don't worry big Jim, I'll be on my best behavior." Clayborne laughed and turning, bowed to Judge Fleming, and then spotting Jesse Grayson for the first time, "Ah, the great reporter is here – hope you enjoy the show."

Is everything ready?" Clayborne sat in one of the bailiff's office chairs.

"It will be now, now that I know the time. Don't worry, I'll see Jake tonight and make sure."

"How about Tressa?" Clayborne asked his attorney.

"Albright's new deputy is bringing her from Forks. She's supposed to be here early tomorrow, so Jake will have to work that out. We assume they'll be bringing her along the main road through Gardiner and then head north."

"Don't assume anything, and remember, have four horses saddled and ready, or your ass is grass."

Seventeen

Jesse sat across from Honiko in the hotel's small dining room. They'd placed their entrée order and while Honiko quietly sipped her tea, Jesse took a large swig of his Rainier beer.

"It will be an exciting day tomorrow. Would you like to attend the trial?"

"I don't think I could see Mr. Clayborne again … I … no, I will stay here … I …"

"Well, I'll be damned, history repeats itself," Sarge Hornsby said, as he entered the room. "Great to see both of you again."

Jesse rose and shook the hand of the trail boss. "Same here, we kind of figured you wouldn't miss the trial."

"Probably would have, as busy as I've been hauling stuff to the mine, but got a subpoena to be a witness, so I had no choice. I'm glad, though, it'll be good to see ole Clayborne get his just desserts."

Sarge grabbed a nearby chair and after giving Honiko a hug, sat down. "Well, I can see you've been busy young man," he

Crescent Gold

said smiling at Honiko. "Must be due pretty soon by the looks of you?"

Honiko blushed and Sarge reached across and patted her hand. "You look beautiful. Like your hair cut short, by the way." He turned to Jesse. "So, why don't you two bring me up-to-date, especially with what's happening at the trial and all. I'm afraid I overslept a wee bit and missed the jury selection."

At the same time Jesse, Sarge and Honiko were talking over a meatloaf dinner at their hotel, Ed Nelson sat in his room at The Palace Hotel reviewing what he knew.

Sitting in the third row of seats in the courtroom he had been able to observe all the actors in the play before him, and he was positive of one thing – Clayborne was too cocky, too carefree, something was up and he guessed the judge, Sheriff Albright and the prosecutor were completely in the dark as to what it was.

He knew Clayborne all too well and he'd stake his life lawyer Osgood and the two ruffians he'd seen with him, were in on whatever plan Clayborne had orchestrated. One thing for sure, Ed knew he'd have to shadow the two hooligans he'd seen with Osgood.

When they'd left Osgood the night before, he'd followed them to a sleazy hotel on Chase Street. The big guy, whom he'd heard Osgood call Jake, looked like a formidable foe. Interestingly, neither he nor the short ugly one had been in court.

This Jake was obviously the "Jake" blurted out in Osgood's ramblings in his room.

Crescent Gold

There were two other things he suspected. If Osgood was in on a getaway plan, he was expecting a reward, and the plot probably involved the map he had rambled on about in his drunken stupor. *Maybe the escape route?*

Eighteen

Stan Clement had only been a Jefferson County Deputy Sheriff for ten months, so with Larry's seniority, he drew the short straw and got the job of bringing Tressa Monroe to Port Townsend. They'd left the prison south of Forks early in the morning, stayed the night at a campsite on the Elwha River, and were now rounding the southern tip of Discovery Bay.

Getting his shackled prisoner in and out of the wagon, giving her limited freedom and privacy when appropriate had taxed his patience, especially at night, when he had had to tie her to a wagon wheel, leaving him to sleep in the open.

He couldn't take any risks. Albright had warned him that Tressa might try something, and she hadn't made it any easier by taunting him every time she had to pee, accusing him of trying to peek. He'd slept less than three hours.

"Should be there in two hours, three at the most," Stan said, checking his watch. It was a few minutes after six.

"No hurry, I'm enjoying the ride. Sure you don't want to stop and let me show you what a good woman can do?" She reached across with her free hand and rubbed his leg.

Crescent Gold

Stan's face reddened, coming close to matching the color of his hair. He ignored her comment and spurred on the horses.

Jake called his current partner "Shorty", but only he could get away with using that moniker. Misjudging his small stature as a sign of weakness had cost one man his life and crippled several others. A quick temper, a hatred of anyone considerably taller, coupled with the strength of men twice his size made Shorty a formidable foe. Throw in his insatiable hunger for the power that money bought, made him the perfect choice for Jake to partner with in implementing the plan to free Tressa Monroe and Spencer Clayborne.

Stan reined in the horses within a few feet of a tree which blocked the roadway. "Damn! Only a few miles to go and this has to happen." He glanced at Tressa. Her bindings looked secure. "No tricks now," he said, swinging down from the buggy's seat.

A rider was coming from the direction of town and stopped his horse near the fallen tree. "Look's like you could use a hand." He dismounted and moved to one end of the trunk, and motioned for Stan to go to the other end.

"On the count of three," the short fellow yelled. "One, two …"

"Wha …" Stan never saw the blow coming, and crumpled to the ground.

Crescent Gold

The short man picked up the trunk end and easily moved it to the side of the road, all the while not saying anything to Tressa who had sat dumbfounded during the attack.

"Listen, if you're going to rob me, I ..." she held up her one free hand. "You picked the wrong buggy." Pointing at Stan she continued, "He's a deputy and I'm his prisoner so I got ..."

"Shut up woman!" He grabbed Stan's legs and pulled him into the brush. "I know all that."

Shorty reached into his jacket and pulled out a knife. "Here, make yourself useful," he said, tossing Tressa the knife, who deftly caught it and began cutting her bindings.

"Well I'll be damned! Keys to my leg chains are in his coat."

Several months in prison had made Tressa leaner and meaner, though she didn't look it. The once leathery-brown complexion was now pale white, but she'd lost fifteen pounds and daily exercise had strengthened the muscles in her five-foot five frame. Gone also was her trademark hair bun, a casualty of strict rules at the prison. Tressa's dark-brown hair was cut short and she was thankful, as the strands of gray that had begun to appear weren't as visible.

She unlocked her chains and jumped to the ground.

Nineteen

Twenty miles to the north, Jesse was finishing a cup of strong coffee and waiting for the waitress to bring the tray he would take to his room. Sarge Hornsby sat opposite Jesse.

"What time does the trial start?"

"Nine sharp, guess I should get over there." Jesse answered.

Four blocks away, Larry carried a tray to Clayborne's cell.

"Eat up Clayborne; we leave for court in less than an hour."

"More of that slop you call oatmeal, I bet, at least the coffee's good." He rose from his bunk and picked up the tray Larry had slid under the cell door. "You goin' to take me to the courthouse, ole buddy?"

"Yep, it'll be my pleasure."

No, it will be mine, Clayborne thought, *it'll be mine*. He checked his watch, tightened his belt – his future inside.

Ed Nelson shivered in the cold and dampness of a typical November morning in Port Townsend. He'd been standing in the doorway across from Jake's hotel since sunup. No sight of either Jake or the shorter man. He checked his watch – eight-

Crescent Gold

fifteen. He didn't want to miss the start of the trial. Maybe he was wrong. Then, there he was …

Jake was alone. Ed waited a few moments in case the other man came, but Jake was hurriedly walking away, toward the courthouse, so he quickly followed.

Following Jake had proven to be no easy task. He stopped and turned at every corner and Ed had to jump into doorways to avoid being seen, or pretend to be looking in a store window. Fortunately, the streets were crowded. *Where the hell is he going?*

Two blocks from the courthouse, Jake turned quickly into an alley that ran between Jefferson and Chase streets. Ed hesitated, and then slowly approached the alley. As luck would have it, a group of three men was coming his way, so he joined them as they passed the alley. Casually glancing to his left he spotted Jake. He was with – it was the short guy, and a woman … she … *Tressa Monroe!*

Twenty

When Jesse arrived at the county courthouse Jim Albright was standing in the hallway talking to Judge Fleming, whose facial expression would have scared a black cat. The mostly one-sided conversation was animated and loud enough that Jesse could hear clearly.

"I don't want any outbursts from Clayborne like we had yesterday. Between you, Bailiff Petersen and your deputy, you better keep him under control."

"I'll try, Judge, but he's a hard one to manage."

"Morning Jim, Judge Fleming," Jesse said as he approached.

Fleming ignored Jesse's greeting. "Don't just try – do it!" He turned and walked around the corner.

"Wow, he's cantankerous this morning," Jesse said, watching Fleming disappear.

"His usual self, I'm afraid. So, ready for the trial?"

"I am. I sent a wire to the paper letting them know it's on schedule for today …"

Crescent Gold

"Howdy, Sheriff!" Sarge Hornsby's boisterous greeting caught Jesse in mid-sentence. "It's going to be a great day. Can hardly wait to see that bastard Clayborne get his."

Albright glanced at the clock on the wall opposite the courtroom door. "Morn' Sarge. Listen, I've got to meet Larry, and you two had better get a seat."

Larry had earlier discussed his route to the courthouse with Sheriff Albright and they decided that to avoid onlookers, he would take a shortcut through the alley that ran behind the jail, go up a block, cross Jefferson Street and then use the alley behind Fraser's Bakery to reach the back door of the courthouse, where Albright would meet him.

As he entered the first alley, he heard a horse's whinny – *strange,* he thought. He'd removed Clayborne's leg irons, but had kept his prisoner's hands bound tightly behind his back. He gave him a push and quickly crossed Jefferson and turned into the second alley.

"C'mon, let's go." As he said this, he looked up to see two men standing outside the back door to Fraser's Bakery. They seemed to be arguing. "Hey, you'll have to get back inside, official business here."

At the same time he again heard a horse whinny. It was behind him. He pulled Clayborne to a halt, and temporarily ignoring the two men who it seemed had disregarded his command, turned to look to his rear. *No one. What the hell's goin' on?* "What th …"

Larry turned back, but too late to avoid the downward arc of a blackjack. The leather-covered club in Jake's hand hit him

Crescent Gold

square on the right temple, sending him crumbling to the ground like a sack of potatoes.

While Shorty left to get the two horses tied up just outside the end of the alley, Tressa moved quickly forward with her two horses. Jake pulled the inert body of Larry into the bakery and laid him next to a gagged, tightly bound and trembling bakery owner.

"Just stay still and we'll be gone soon," Jake said to the frightened man.

"How about the deputy? He looks dead." Clayborne asked, struggling to get out of his bindings.

"Don't know, but we've only got a minute or so, here, this will help." He handed Clayborne a knife. "Let's go, the horses should be ready."

"Won't we be seen?" Free of his restraints, he followed Jake out the door.

"No. Just across the street the alley leads to a park, and on the other side of the park is a road that leads east. Once on the road, we should be in the clear. Most everyone in town is over at the courthouse waiting for your grand entrance." Jake paused. "This was your plan, wasn't it?"

"Yeah, but I didn't know where you'd be. Yeah, my plan, you're right, guess I'm just overly excited," Clayborne said, tossing the last piece of rope.

They stepped outside to find Tressa and Shorty already mounted. Clayborne smiled widely at Tressa and blew her a kiss.

Crescent Gold

"Let's get out of here, you can smooch later – and Clayborne, that money had better be where you say it is."

Ed Nelson had no doubts that Jake and the short man had somehow freed Tressa Monroe and that the three of them were up to no good, and it probably involved Clayborne.

He'd retreated across the street and was standing in the entryway to the Mercantile. Ed realized they could be gone by now, down the alley to the next street, and was about to venture out when he spotted Albright's Deputy and Clayborne crossing Jefferson. They went into the alley.

When Tressa Monroe came around the corner with two horses and entered the alley, he guessed what had happened, and ran across the street, but instead of looking in the alley, he held back and listened. Clayborne's voice was unmistakable.

"All right, let's get out of here, before they realize what happened. "Tressa and I will meet you in Irondale, in the grove behind Chester's Livery on Main Street, as planned."

Then a second voice. "Hold on there, Clayborne, we'll ride together or not at all."

"Put the gun away, Jake. Okay, I was just suggesting we'd be less obvious if we split up. Don't worry you'll get your money …"

"Forget that. We ride together!"

"What about the lawyer?" another male voice asked.

Must be the short guy, Ed thought, straining to hear.

"He knows where we're meeting; he'll have to get there on his own, and if he doesn't, it's his tough luck."

Crescent Gold

Ed heard the noise of horses and riders moving away. He hesitated, then looked around the corner. They were gone.

Crescent Gold

Twenty-One

Judge Fleming's bailiff softly knocked on the heavy oak door.

"Come!"

Bailiff Jensen straightened his cravat, buttoned the top button on his vest and entered the Judge's chambers.

"Well?" Fleming walked from behind his desk. "Are they here?"

The bailiff shook his head.

"Damn-nation! Get Osgood and Albright in here right now!"

"They're right here, along with Mr. Lasley," he stepped aside and Albright, Osgood and the Prosecuting Attorney walked in.

"Sheriff, where the hell's Clayborne, it's ten after nine?"

"That's what I'd like to know, your Honor," Osgood said, sarcastically.

"Listen Osgood, if you're pulling something …"

"Hold on, Sheriff, I'm just as befuddled as you are. Probably just …"

Fleming cut Osgood short. "Sheriff, go see what the delay is."

Crescent Gold

Jim Albright sensed something had gone terribly wrong. He followed the route Larry and Clayborne should have taken. He noticed the door to the bakery was ajar, but hurried on. At the jail, the cell was empty, so he knew they'd gone – but, where? Trying not to panic, he retraced his steps to the courthouse. When he passed the rear of the bakery, he noticed the door was still open, and something told him to go in.

Albright removed the gag from Fraser. "How long ago did they leave?"

"About ten minutes. I think Larry's dead."

Albright knelt down and felt for a pulse. "Weak, but he's alive."

He untied Fraser's hands. "Do you have a telephone?"

"Yes, on the wall, out by the cash register."

"Listen, I'm going to telephone the hospital and then run back to the courthouse. You wait here, and you might have them check you over too."

"I will, and by the way, sheriff, there was a woman with them."

Ten minutes later Judge Fleming, Lasley and Osgood heard that Clayborne had escaped and Albright believed he must have had several accomplices, one a woman.

Osgood listened intently, feigning surprise, but all the while he was getting increasingly nervous. If he was to meet Clayborne tonight, as planned, he needed to get going. The plan was for him to meet Clayborne in Irondale, then, after paying off the two hooligans, Clayborne would show him the

Crescent Gold

map and he, Tressa Monroe and Clayborne would travel together to the site of the treasure.

"Osgood, Osgood! Are you listening to me?" Judge Fleming screamed. "Until the sheriff finds Clayborne, and he'd better, you are dismissed."

Albright had also tried listening to Fleming as he berated not only him, but all the law enforcement for miles around, attorney Osgood and anyone else he could conjure up for blame. Like Osgood, Albright's thoughts had been focused elsewhere, and he was eager to get out of the courthouse, see how Larry was doing, find out what happened to Deputy Stan and his prisoner, figure where Clayborne had gone and hopefully, how to recapture him and arrest those that helped him escape.

Fleming postponed the trial and Albright headed for the hospital. At the bottom of the courthouse steps he collided with Osgood. "Oops, sorry Taylor, guess we're both in a hurry."

"That's okay, I wasn't watching either. Good luck with the search. Hope you find Clayborne and that girlfriend of his. I hear she's a real pistol, typical of all that Monroe clan, if you ask me."

Twenty-Two

For a second or two, Ed Nelson considered going to the livery, getting a horse and following Clayborne. It would have been impossible. *I've blown it! Damn.*

Then he remembered! It hit him like a ton of bricks.

He hurried to the courthouse, arriving just in time to witness Jim Albright and Taylor Osgood have their collision. He hesitated, then crouched down behind a hooded-buggy and watched, as they talked briefly and then Albright headed down the street, away from where Nelson was standing. Osgood looked around and then walked across the street. Nelson realized none too soon, the lone horse-drawn buggy on the street was probably Osgood's.

He stood up before Osgood could see he had been hiding. "Lawyer Osgood, how's the trial coming?"

Osgood nodded at Nelson. "Not so good, I'm afraid. It seems my client has ... ah, shall we say, 'flown the coop'."

"Well I'll be. Too bad. Ah ... escaped from the jail, did he?"

"It appears so. Listen, it's good to see you again, but I've got to get going."

"Yes, yes, I understand," Nelson said. "Good luck. Say, could you give me a ride to the livery, I'm late to meet a client."

Osgood hesitated. He needed to get to his room, get a few supplies and his gun, and head south to Irondale, but he didn't want to appear over anxious. "Fine – livery's on the way to my rooms, climb on."

As they rode down Jefferson Street, they passed Jesse and Sarge Hornsby. Nelson looked away.

Twenty-Three

"There's Osgood and that fellow I saw him with at the tavern," Jesse said to Sarge, as the buggy passed by.

"You know, there's something about that other guy that still bugs me. He reminds me of someone and I can't put my finger on it. Oh well." Sarge put his arm around Jesse. "So, what do we do now? I've got orders for supplies to take to Copper City, and I bet you don't have all the time in the world, before you have to head back, especially with Honiko's condition."

"I think we should check with the sheriff. Before he left, he told me he was going to the hospital, maybe we can catch him there?" Jesse said. "I can stay a few more days, but it sounds like if they don't catch Clayborne, I might as well head back to Frisco."

"I'll go with you to the hospital, but unless there's an emergency, I'm leaving for Quilcene on the morning train." He buttoned his coat. "Brr, it's getting cold, hope I don't have snow to deal with on the trail to Copper City, those burros are sure-footed, but they can be stubborn."

Crescent Gold

After Albright learned that Larry had sustained a skull fracture, was still unconscious, but had a good chance at a full recovery, he'd headed to his room above the jail, packed some clothes and saddled his horse. He had no idea where Clayborne had gone, so his first priority was to see what had happened to his new deputy. If Tressa Monroe was free, she'd either tricked Stan, or more likely, been aided in her escape. He swung up into the saddle and then – "son-of-a-bitch!" he said out loud, then, "Tressa Monroe."

He said to himself, *that old coot Osgood.*

Stan would have to wait. He snapped the reins and gave his horse a light kick. Hopefully he'd find Osgood before he left town. He was now positive the lawyer was in on the escape and if he shadowed him, Osgood would lead him to Clayborne.

Crescent Gold

Jefferson County Courthouse – Port Townsend

Crescent Gold

Part Two

Crescent Gold

Crescent Gold

Twenty-Four

1482 A D

The winter had been kind to the S'Klallam people, but Kaiahan and the tribal elders knew the Guiding Spirit that had watched over them might not be so benevolent in the new year.

At a meeting of the elders, Kaiahan argued that a few of the men should return to the great lake and determine whether they could rebuild Tien-ah, and just as important, could the treasured pendants be recovered, for they would need them for trade and for tribal rituals.

Kaiahan knew if his judgment prevailed, he would assuredly be selected to lead the expedition, and even though O'Wota was with child, he would have no choice but to agree.

The wall in the main cave now showed Kaiahan's rendition of the story of the tribe's journey from their former winter home. It had taken him many days. *Some day*, he thought as he had worked, *I will have a son to help me and he will learn the*

Crescent Gold

meaning of the frog, the water bird, the arrow and other symbols, as I learned from my father.

He had been fortunate to finish as early as he did, for it was S'Klallam tradition to cease all work during what were called "the black days." These were the days when the life-giving sun sank lower in the sky each midday and darkness prevailed. Although many days of harsh weather remained, the tribe took solace that the return of warm weather was forthcoming. The S'Klallam came to associate this time of year with birth and imminent renewal. Not by accident, many new additions to the tribe occurred nine moons later.

The days of darkness had lasted longer this year because the tribe was high in the mountains, living in their cave dwellings rather than beside the great lake. Kaiahan hoped to use this fact to his advantage this evening when he pleaded with the elders. Although he'd become passionate about completing the wall painting, he prayed the map to their former winter home would never have to be used, that they could return and rebuild before another generation passed, memories of their history faded and the route to the lake and the treasure it held, forgotten.

He heard the soft shuffling of moccasins and then a light touch on his shoulder. "Come, my love, it is time. The tribe awaits you."

Kaiahan reached back and took his mate's hand. "I know. Their decision will shape our lives and those of our child. I am worried they may feel the wrath of the great Storm God is still too strong for us to return." He rose from the small fire in the cave they shared with three other families and gently pushed the jet black hair away from her brown eyes, then moved his hand down to encircle her swollen stomach.

"What happens if they are right and we do not return? I must be here for you and the child."

O'Wota glanced up at her mate. "Only the Guiding Spirit knows the answer to that, only he will determine your fate and the fate of our tribe. Hurry now, the elders are getting impatient."

Twenty-Five

1907 AD

Snow in November was not unusual in the temperate climate of the Olympic Peninsula, but always a surprise at low altitudes where rain was the norm in late autumn.

Jim Albright had figured the lawyer would either be at one of his favorite watering holes, The Black Swan or The Brown Lantern, and barring that, he'd be at his room. This assumed he hadn't already left town. No one had seen him at either of the taverns.

Osgood's buggy wasn't tied to the post and Albright started to question his assumptions. He tethered his horse behind the Stetson Apartments, brushed the snowflakes off his coat, and climbed the steps to Osgood's room.

He listened at the door, but heard nothing. He knocked. No answer. *Now what?* he thought.

Walking out the front door, he almost collided with Widow Kramer, who was sweeping the accumulated snow off the steps. "Ooops, sorry Mrs. Kramer."

Crescent Gold

"Why Sheriff, what you a-doin' here?" the elderly widow said. "You'd better head for home, looks like this white stuffs gonna stick around. Gets dark early this time a year, ya know."

"Thanks Mrs. Kramer, and you shouldn't be out here in this cold, either."

"Part of the job, ya know. Since mister died, it's been pretty much up to me to manage this old place. Gotta keep the tenants happy."

"Ah ... speaking of tenants, I was looking for Taylor Osgood."

"Oh, that big bag of wind. Was here bout ten minutes ago, just after the snow started comin down."

Albright waited for the old lady to continue, but instead she returned to her sweeping.

"Do you know where he is?"

"He's not in his room."

Albright tried to be patient. "I know – do you know where he is?" he repeated.

"Nope, but he went that direction in his buggy." She pointed south, down the road.

"Funny thing too, just afore you came, a stranger rode by going fast in the same direction."

"Thank you Mrs. Kramer." She nodded slightly, grunted and returned to her sweeping.

Albright climbed in his saddle and headed south. *Thank God the snow had been falling*, he thought. *The ruts left by the buggy wheels should be easy to follow.*

Crescent Gold

Jesse Grayson was frustrated. The main focus of his planned story, Spencer Clayborne had escaped to who knew where. He had no idea of the whereabouts of Jim Albright, Sarge Hornsby had decided to leave for Quilcene in the morning, and he had a very pregnant wife two floors up, who was likely wondering where her husband was. Where he was, was in the lobby of the Carlton Manor, trying to decide whether to call it quits and return to San Francisco, or stay put in Port Townsend for a day or so and see what happened. He'd earlier telephoned the *Chronicle* and updated his editor, but got no help in making the decision.

"Well, you look like crap!" His head jerked up to see Sarge, legs spread apart, hands on his hips, Pince-Nez glasses halfway down his nose, standing in the Carlton's entry doorway.

"Thought you were going to go pack so you could catch the first train tomorrow." Jesse said, rising to greet Hornsby.

"I was, but changed my mind. Larry's come around and he asked me to see what happened to Stan. Unless this damn snow delays me, I'm leaving within the hour."

"But Sarge, it'll be dark in a couple hours and the snow is coming down pretty steady."

"I know, I'm not stupid. "Listen, young friend, I've traveled in worse, and I figure if Albright's new deputy is still alive, it's worth the gamble, and besides, I owe Jim and Larry a favor or two. He put his arm around Jesse. "I could use a partner – want to come along? Might be a story in it – should only take a day. Clayborne's long gone. Got an extra horse outside, saddled and ready …"

"You're crazy, and I guess I am too."

Twenty-Six

Tressa rode alongside Spencer Clayborne, followed closely by Jake and Shorty. What had begun as a light, powdery dusting had now turned into a heavy, constant snowfall, blanketing the narrow road and slowing their pace.

She looked back. The two henchmen were falling behind. "Spencer," she whispered.

"Yeah." He said quietly looking ahead, and trying to remain on the trail in the face of decreased visibility. "Don't ask me again how far. Christ, I'm doing all I can just to follow the road." He pulled his jacket collar closer to his neck.

"I know. They're out of earshot right now," she said, turning slightly and looking behind. "When we gonna dump these two rubes?"

"Shhhh, they'll hear you. I want to get to Irondale first, and then we'll take care of them and head west."

"You got the key to the box?"

"You bet, you got the gu ..."

Crescent Gold

"Hey! What the hell you two yakkin' about up there?" Jake said, pulling closer to Tressa.

Clayborne reined in his mount. "Tressa was just asking about how long to Irondale. For the fifth time! Anyway, I figure in about another ten to fifteen minutes, we should be there."

"And the four hundred smackers are there, huh?"

"Yup, right where I stashed em. Then you two can hightail it and Tressa and me will head for Quilcene."

"How about Osgood, you wait'n for him to show?"

Clayborne turned in his saddle. "What do you think?"

Taylor Osgood was no rookie, as most people thought, in fact when he wasn't drunk he was a good lawyer and in his youth, had hiked and ridden all over the backcountry of the Olympic Peninsula. This night, however, it was taking all his concentration and skill just to stay on the snow crusted dirt road. *Thank God I haven't had a drink,* he'd thought on more than one occasion. At every curve he had to slow to a crawl or the buggy wheels skidded precariously close to the ditch that paralleled the gravel road. No one would find him if he went off the road, he was alone.

Beyond the ditch stood rows of giant sentinels that on any other night would have presented a picture perfect Christmas scene – this night it was eerie, foreboding.

Now with the snow coming down even harder, he'd slowed his rig to a snail's pace, even on straight stretches. A few minutes after slowing down, he heard a horse whinny. *Someone else as crazy as I am, maybe I'm not alone.* Then he heard it again, only closer. Glancing through the thick flakes he swore the shape of a horse and rider were visible.

He reined in his horse. "Hey back there." No answer.

"What the ..."

Out of nowhere a giant shadow loomed before him.

The buggy wheel ruts were beginning to fill in and Jim Albright feared they'd be all but gone soon. However, the road he was traveling on led only to Irondale and then Chimacum, so he guessed as long as he could make out the road, he was still following Osgood.

There was also a set of tracks to follow. The four-legged variety, and by the look of the horseshoe impressions, whoever it was couldn't be too far ahead. Albright recalled Mrs. Kramer's comment and figured it must be the rider she saw. *Following Osgood, too?*

Instead of going up Main Street, Clayborne rode behind the Irondale General Store and to the rear of the livery stable. "Snow's stopped," he said reining in his mount. "Tie up over there and give me a few minutes. Tressa, you stay here with Jake and Shorty, I'll be right back."

Jake chortled. "You got to be kidding. I'm coming with you. She can stay here with Shorty." Unseen by Clayborne, Jake gave a slight nod and winked at Shorty.

"All right, come on."

Clayborne walked around to the front of the livery stable. There was a light in the one window that faced Main Street. He knocked on the door. He knocked again.

Crescent Gold

"Hold your horses, I'll be there."

The door swung open to reveal a gnarled, wry-eyebrowed old man, his frame so contorted he appeared hunchbacked. He looked up. "Well I'll be damned, Spencer Clayborne. Thought you was in jail up in Townsend."

"I was Chet, got out early. Listen, I need to have that box I left with you last year."

"You bet. Preciate the money, by the way. Hold on, I'll be right back."

Momentarily, he returned with a metal box. "Here, it was just where you left it."

Clayborne set the box down and removed his belt. "Got a knife, Chet?"

"You bet, here." Chet opened a pocketknife and handed it to Clayborne.

Clayborne slit the seam of the belt and removed a key, then using the key; he opened the box and reached in.

"Thanks Chet, here's the other thirty smackers I promised. I'll be off, thanks again for keeping this." Clayborne put the metal box under his arm and went out the door. Jake was close behind.

Clayborne returned to the rear of the livery where Tressa and Shorty waited with the horses. Shorty glared at Clayborne. "It's about time, damn cold out here." Then to Jake, "Let's get our money and go somewhere warm. I could use a drink."

"I need some light," Clayborne said, moving under the lone light that hung from the corner of the building. He reopened the box and withdrew a roll of bills.

Crescent Gold

"Let's make it the whole wad," said Shorty, in a threatening tone. "Else this lady of yours might get roughed up." He grabbed Tressa from behind, his forearm pressing against her throat.

"Easy there – whatever I've got, you're welcome to it." He unrolled the wad and began counting, but noticed out of the corner of his eye that Jake now held a gun.

"There's just over six hundred." He handed the bills to Jake, who took them and smiled.

"Sure that's all, let me have a look," Jake said, cramming the money in his jacket pocket, stuffing the gun in his waistband, and grabbing the box from Clayborne.

"Well, well, what do we have here?" He removed and unfolded a piece of paper and studied it for a moment. "Looks like a bunch of Injun pictures – um, must be important for you to have hidden it." He drew his gun and pointed it at Clayborne. "Fess up, what's all this gobbledygook mean?"

"Jake!" Shorty yelled, "Somebody's coming."

Twenty-Seven

When the snow abated and the Irondale city sign came into view, Taylor Osgood sighed deeply. The large bull elk jumping across his path had scared him to his core, but he decided the rider he'd seen behind him was likely another elk, or a mirage caused by the snow and his weariness. He'd pushed on hoping to catch up with Clayborne and the others.

Four people were standing behind the livery stable. Jake was near Clayborne, while Shorty had his arm tightly wrapped around a woman he assumed was Tressa Monroe.

Jake spoke first. "Why Osgood, glad you joined us. Just in time for the party."

"It's not like you waited for me." He glanced at Tressa and Shorty as he climbed down. "What's going on?"

"What's going on is that Clayborne here has decided to graciously give us more than the measly four hundred you promised and was about to explain what's so all-fired important about this," he said, waving the unfolded sheet of paper.

Crescent Gold

Osgood walked to Jake and reached for the paper. "Let's see." He was pretty sure he was looking at the map to the lake and the treasure trove, but moved over under the light, feigning recognition. "Can't see much in this light, but it just looks like a bunch of animal drawings? Why don't you take your money and go?"

"Oh you'd like that – something's fishy here, you're too eager to have us gone." Jake grabbed the paper and pushed Osgood away. "Shorty, why don't you see what Miss Tressa's hiding under that cute little outfit, in fact, we'd all like to see."

"C'mon Jake," Clayborne said, "leave her alone, give me back the paper and the box and I'll show you."

"That's more like it," Jake said. "Shorty, let her come over here by Osgood. There's some rope in my saddlebag, tie the two of them up."

"But I …"

Jake slapped Osgood across the face. "Shut up you old drunkard."

Jake didn't notice Clayborne reach into the box, remove the false bottom, pull out a pistol, while at the same time nodding at Tressa.

The first shot from the 22 caliber, double barrel Derringer hit Jake squarely between the eyes. The pistol was small but packed a big wallop, and most of Jake's face was gone, much of it spattering Osgood. The bullet from Tressa's Browning automatic ripped through Shorty's back, just below his neck and he toppled forward into the slushy mud. Osgood stood trembling, then sank to his knees and threw up.

Crescent Gold

"Ole Deputy Stan's gun came in handy, huh. C'mon, Chester and half the town must have heard that."

Tressa nodded. "What about him?" She was pointing at Osgood, "Can't have him yapping about."

"He's not going to tell anyone, he'd go to jail. But if you think it's a risk, pump one into him, and let's go. Come to think of it, he does know about the map – actually, he's seen it now, probably guessed the location, seeing he's been around these parts for a while…"

"No, I won't tell about the lake… I …oh my … G …"

"Look Spence, he's pissed his pants." She leveled the gun at the lawyer. Then, "naw, he won't tell anybody, let's get out of here."

Ed Nelson had watched the drama play out before him and only when Spencer Clayborne and Tressa Monroe galloped by heading west, away from town did he consider leaving his hiding place in a thick stand of pine trees. He started to run to Osgood, but quickly pulled back when several men came tearing around the corner of the livery stable. He drew back even farther in the shadows when a lone rider came down the road. A rider he easily recognized as Jim Albright. Nelson had tied his mount to one of the trees and hoped he'd stay quiet in spite of the ensuing noise, so hunkering down, he strained to hear the conversations, wishing he could have followed Clayborne. *The lake, what lake?*

Albright reined in next to the circle of men that surrounded the grizzly scene. In the center, a trembling Taylor Osgood. Nelson heard Albright call to the stable owner.

Crescent Gold

"Chet, you see what happened?"

"Sheriff! You sure arrived on cue," Chet hollered. "No, heard the shots and came running just in time to see two riders heading that way." He pointed west. "One for sure was Spencer Clayborne. The other coulda been a woman."

Albright walked over to Osgood, who Nelson could see was covered with blood and gore. Nelson strained to hear. "You get shot?" Albright asked.

A still trembling Osgood looked up. "No, I'm covered with Jake's … ah … Jake's …"

"I got it, Osgood. You're under arrest, by the way." He turned and walked to one of the dead men. "This one Jake?"

Osgood nodded. "The other one's called Shorty. Tressa Monroe shot him, Clayborne shot Jake."

Albright turned to Chet. "Could you get some blankets or sheets and cover these guys, we're liable to have more townsfolk show up, and Chet, I'd appreciate you keeping everybody away. Also, would you have someone get a towel so Osgood can clean up. He's beginning to stink." Albright turned back to Osgood and Nelson heard him say, "Now, let's start at the beginning." Albright grabbed Osgood under the arm, pulled him erect and moved away, closer to the livery stable.

Nelson couldn't hear anything that was now being said, as Albright was facing away from him and Osgood was barely talking above a whisper. He was in a quandary, stay put and try to learn as much as he could, or sneak away and try to catch up to Clayborne. It was gnawing at him, *what lake?* From what he'd heard earlier, Jake had thought Osgood knew.

I'll stay put.

Twenty-Eight

The bodies of Jake and Shorty had been carried into Chester's Irondale Livery, and Jim Albright was taking a break from questioning Taylor Osgood, who was tied to one of the wheels of his buggy that had been pulled inside the livery.

He'd learned that on Clayborne's second meeting with Osgood, his court-appointed attorney had been pulled into the escape plan, somewhat easily, Albright concluded from the sound of it. The carrot had been the promise of enormous wealth, generated by the sharing of a treasure, the location of which was supposedly detailed on a map in Clayborne's possession. Chet told Albright about the box, so he assumed the map was in the box the livery owner had been paid to hold for Clayborne.

Osgood's first mission had been to contact Jake Porter. Clayborne and Jake had been partners in some shady deals before and, although his loyalty often was overshadowed by greed, Clayborne felt he was the right man for this job. The payment was to be four hundred dollars, which would be

Crescent Gold

shared if Jake needed additional help. Shorty had been recruited.

Rescuing Tressa Monroe and bringing her to Port Townsend became Shorty's assignment. Clayborne had figured that if he was not able to escape, at least Tressa would be free, and thereby not be forced to testify at his trial.

The plans had proceeded without a hitch until Osgood arrived in Irondale. Jake and Shorty had obviously decided their services were worth more than four hundred dollars and, as Osgood explained, Jake found the hidden map. As it turned out, however, the tables became quickly reversed when Shorty momentarily took his eyes off Tressa, and Clayborne pulled a gun out of the box. Osgood had expected to be shot.

Albright had been able to piece the rest of the story together, and now as he enjoyed a fresh pipe, he pondered his next questions and again confronted his prisoner.

"Tell me more about the map." He purposely directed some smoke in Osgood's face.

"Clayborne is convinced it leads to a treasure of gold pendants at the site of an ancient Indian village," coughing and turning his head.

Albright knew about the pendants Clayborne and Menucci had smuggled from the cave above the mine shaft. *Can these pendants be from the same cave?*

"Where'd he get the map?"

"Said he copied it from the wall in some cave near Copper City," Osgood said. "It was in the box that held the money, and as it turned out, with the gun he used to kill Jake."

Crescent Gold

"How did he know it was the map to some hidden treasure?" he said, his tone skeptical, but now having confirmed his assumption about the source of the pendants.

Osgood was contemplative for a minute. "He never really explained, but he did mention a book he got from the library and he was pretty convincing about the cave drawings. I was won over when I read in the *Leader* about the gold pendants he'd found."

"So where is the site – near this lake you talk about, I gather?"

"Not just any lake, my belief is that the site is at Lake Crescent." He paused, seeing Albright's questioning stare. "I'm sure it's Lake Crescent because in the brief look I got, I saw a figure I've seen before in local Indian paintings, the god the S'Klallam call 'Storm King', and Lake Crescent lies below Storm King Mountain."

"If you're right about Lake Crescent, that's probably where they're headed. But where on the lake, it's huge, not even a road to most of it."

"You'd need Clayborne's map for that."

Crescent Gold

Twenty-Nine

The elders had agreed with Kaiahan, and in two days, weather permitting, he and two other men would journey to Tien-ah; the site of the tribe's devastated winter lodgings. The trip would be arduous but necessary. The S'Klallam elders knew they'd been fortunate to have a mild winter and would need to either rebuild near the old site, or move to another sheltered location.

Kaiahan was apprehensive on two fronts: primary was the possibility of not returning in time for the birth of his first child, and also the prospect that he might not return at all. In the likelihood of the second event, he realized that of the remaining men, only two knew the meaning of the symbols in his wall painting. These men were old, which meant that in two or three years, there might not be anyone to interpret his recent painting, and therefore, both the record of their trek and the route back to the great lake and the treasure of pendants would be lost. None of the women knew the meanings – knowledge of the ancient symbols was restricted to the men of the tribe, and for centuries, the males of Kaiahan's clan.

Crescent Gold

It had also occurred to him that if he didn't return he would not be able to teach his son and the sacred right would pass to another line, as Kaiahan was the last living male in his clan. He decided he would break tradition and risk the wrath of the elders.

O'Wota and another woman were gathering wood for their fires. Kaiahan waited at the cave entrance and when they returned he asked his mate to leave the branches for the other women to take in the cave, and follow him.

He led her back down the trail to a secluded spot beneath a large cedar. From under his outer garment he removed a role of birch bark and several sticks with charred ends.

"I must teach you the meaning of the sacred symbols used in my paintings," he said, motioning for her to sit.

She looked up at him with wondering eyes. "It is forbidden. You will be punished and I will be shunned, perhaps even made to leave the tribe."

"We must take the risk." He unrolled the bark and while the sunlight remained, told and sketched for O'Wota the meaning of the symbols.

"Both the feather and the wolf tracks indicate direction. The feather is used for shorter distances, those that take less than a day. The small stones are for very short distances, and when shown with an arrow, each stone is twenty paces." He hesitated and looked at his mate for a sign of understanding, and continued. "A frog is a water animal, so a drawing of a frog means the location of water. A water bird, like ducks, geese or heron indicates a large body of water, or when drawn next to a

Crescent Gold

river, means the river is long." He paused again. "A water bird may also be used to indicate a spring – often symbolizing fertility. Herons are only used to represent water surrounded by land."

He went on. "The drawing of a hand represents the presence of man. Two crossed hands means an encampment. River lines are drawn as they might look, and mountains or hills are drawn as lumps or like this for a very tall mountain." He drew an inverted "V".

"It is important to observe the feet of the water bird. If they are narrow, then the body of water is narrow, if round …"

O'Wota interrupted. "So if the feet are like this …," she used one of the sticks and drew a heron with curved feet, standing amid a circle, and next to the circle, a large inverted V with the figure of a man above it, "it would be as shown on your cave drawing, as meaning our village of Tien-ah on the Great Water, below Storm God's mountain?"

He nodded and smiled. "Yes, and the wolf tracks, feathers and stones show the way from this mountain."

Thirty

As much as Albright wanted to leave quickly and follow Clayborne, he knew he had to take Osgood to the Port Townsend jail, arrange for the burial of Jake and Shorty and hopefully find one of his deputies healthy enough to go with him.

He also knew that Frank Fischer ran a stage line between Gardiner and Lake Crescent with a stop in Sequim and Port Angeles. If he could get to Port Townsend tonight, travel by horse to Gardiner in the morning and take the stagecoach, he had a chance to get to the southeast shore of the lake before Clayborne and Monroe, who he assumed, would be traveling over rough terrain.

When Ben agreed to bury Jake and Shorty, Albright tied his horse behind Osgood's buggy, roped Osgood in the buggy's right seat and headed for Port Townsend.

Nelson had faced much the same dilemma as Albright, leave quickly and hope to catch up to Clayborne, or shadow the sheriff and hope he'd learned enough from Osgood to know where Clayborne was going. When Albright took Osgood into

Crescent Gold

the livery, Nelson left his shelter and ran to the opposite side of the livery from where the bodies lay.

Fortunately the livery's thin walls and Osgood's proximity to the wall allowed Nelson to hear all of the conversation with Albright. Clayborne was headed to Lake Crescent in search of a cache of gold pendants. He quietly returned to his former hiding place, untied his horse and headed northwest, now under clear skies. If he was lucky, he would catch the first coach in the morning from Gardiner. *The Warrior will get his revenge and a nice profit, too*, he thought as he put his horse in a gallop.

Sarge Hornsby and Jesse Grayson were hunkered down for the night, about three miles north of Discovery Bay. The snow had stopped, but it was bitter cold and the horse's puffs of exhausted air quickly crystallized. It had been slow going along the narrow, icy road.

Rolled up in a blanket, Sarge snored loudly, oblivious to the cold and Jesse's shivering, who by now thought he was doubly crazy for coming with Sarge.

Since leaving Port Townsend, they'd encountered no one. Of course, had Deputy Stan been lying by the road, he would have been covered by snow. Sarge had decided to push on to at least Gardiner before giving up, and he argued clear skies in the morning would give them an advantage.

Thirty-One

While Jesse lay shivering next to Sarge, Spencer Clayborne and Tressa Monroe were enjoying the heat from their fire and eating the last of the hard boiled eggs and venison jerky Tressa had been able to bring. They'd gotten about a mile north of Gardiner before snow, darkness and exhaustion had convinced Clayborne to stop for the night. In the morning they'd need to find food for themselves and the horses if they stood a chance of reaching Lake Crescent before darkness once again set in.

Clayborne assumed Sheriff Albright was not far behind if he'd figured out where they were headed, and too late he realized leaving Osgood alive might prove to have been a very bad idea.

He tossed a handful of egg shells in the fire. "Where the hell did you get these eggs, they're almost rotten?"

"Albright's deputy had 'm with him."

"If they'd a been colored I'd a thought they were last year's Easter eggs."

Tressa threw a piece of wood on the fire and ignored his remark. "You're sure you know the way?"

Crescent Gold

He stared at the fire, as if mesmerized by the flames that were trying to consume the shells. "What's it worth to ya," he finally answered, reaching around and fondling her breast.

She pulled away. "Damn it, Spence, be serious. We'll have time for that later."

"Okay, but you can't blame a guy for trying." He reached into his jacket pocket and pulled out the map, holding it close to the fire. "Let me show you."

He spread out the drawing. "First, what does this look like?"

"Like the gold pendants we had – the bird is the same and that V shape looks like a mountain."

"And not just any mountain, it's Storm King Mountain. I discovered that the heron is the Indian's symbol for a lake and that figure above, what you correctly see as a mountain, is their Storm King God. So, Storm King, a lake, it's got to be Lake Crescent."

Tressa sighed. "But that doesn't pin down any location, even if you're right."

"That's where these other symbols come in, see the two crossed hands. That indicates a village of men, and see the feathers and stones?"

"Yeah, but …"

"No buts – okay, what's this look like?" he said pointing to the right side of the drawing. "Look close."

"Ah … could be the where the Quilcene River flows around Iron Mountain, ah … this could be Copper Creek – near Tubal Cain Mine." She looked up. "By God it is, it's Iron Mountain where the cave is and …"

Crescent Gold

"Where I found the gold pendants! Now, the wolf tracks and feathers point the way. Look, they lead right to the heron that's by the crossed hands. And guess what, the number of stones after that last feather I'm sure add up to the distance from this symbol." He pointed to what looked like a human nose.

"What's that? It reminds me of that schnozz on Osgood."

"It wasn't in the book, so we'll have to figure that out when we get there, now c'mon give a guy a little lovin."

Thirty-Two

Most of Lake Crescent was accessible only by boat and trail. A road on the south shore was planned, but construction had not started. Six months ago, The Marymere Hotel on Barnes Point had opened. It was the first hotel built on the south shore. Guests arrived by boat, usually having traveled first by coach from Sequim, Port Angeles or Forks.

Another hotel, The Log Cabin Hotel, was built on the north shore at Piedmont, which was at the end of the road from Port Crescent on the Strait of Juan de Fuca.

The builders of the Marymere selected Barnes Point for their hotel site, as the point was located on the narrowest part of the lake and at the base of the western shoulder of Mount Storm King. The hotel was less than a mile from the spectacular Marymere Falls.

The Barnes' family building contractor had run into some difficulty at first. An old S'Klallam Indian who lived near La Poel claimed the proposed site was on sacred ground, that a village of his ancestors had once been located there. The

Crescent Gold

county, eager for the income from tourism, ignored the man's claims, and construction was started.

One of the unique features of the log and wood frame hotel was a five-sided bay window with a correspondingly shaped dormer above. The view of the lake and surrounding mountains from the dormer window was astounding. Even more amazing was the sight cast by the midday sun on certain winter days. When the sun was at its zenith the shadow projected onto the south shore of the lake by the shape of Storm King Mountain resembled a large nose.

The stagecoach had pulled out from Frank Fisher's office in Sequim on schedule. The two men bound for Port Angeles had yakked all the way, and Ed Nelson, finally alone and oblivious to the rough road, slept all the way to the pier at Lake Crescent. Upon arrival, the stagecoach driver told him the boat would be docking in ten minutes.

While he waited, Ed idly chatted with the coach driver, Charley Parkhurst.

"Is this the last coach today from Port Angeles?"

"No, there's another later today that left from Gardiner, stopped in Sequim, then he stops in Port Angeles and Fairholm. He stays here for the night and I head back in an hour, empty or not, to be in Sequim for the morning run."

"So that coach get's here in about two hours?" Nelson asked.

"Yup." He put his whip under his arm and pulled out his pocketwatch. "About noon."

Crescent Gold

Nelson contemplated his situation. He felt confident that he was the first to arrive at Lake Crescent, but that being said, he knew without Clayborne and his map, he had no clue what to do next.

"Where do most people stay?" he asked the driver.

"At either the Marymere or the Log Cabin, unless you want to rough it at Ovington's Resort. I hear tell ole Avery Singer is thinking about building a tavern on the south shore, near the Marymere, but nothing's started yet, because that old Indian, Chetzemoka that caused trouble for the Barnes' is at it again."

A sharp horn blast signaled the arrival of the ferry boat.

"Thanks for the help. If the boat goes to all three spots, where does it dock first?"

"Marymere." He looked askance at Nelson. "Where you staying? I kinda figured you musta had a room, coming this far, and all."

"No – but, I'll try the Marymere."

Sarge and Jesse had been traveling the road north from Discovery Bay to Gardiner for about an hour when Sarge's sharp eyes caught sight of a pair of boots sticking out from a clump of tall grass.

"Look Jesse!" He dismounted and ran to the grassy area, followed quickly by Jesse.

As Sarge knelt down Jesse heard a soft groan. "My God Sarge, he's alive."

"Not for long, by the looks of that head wound," Sarge said. "Run back to my horse and get my blankets, and in my bags, there's a medical kit. Oh, and bring the canteen."

Crescent Gold

Sarge wrapped one blanket around Stan, the other he folded and put under Stan's head. "Pour some water on that rag," he told Jesse, as he removed a brown bottle and roll of cloth from the bag. "Looks like a pretty bad cut on his head, but I don't see any other wounds. Guess being out in the cold overnight would be enough to finish off most men.

Jesse squatted down next to Sarge. "What do we do now?"

"Well, while I nurse this guy, you get some wood and get a fire goin – we'll all feel better after that I 'spect."

Jim Albright smelt the smoke before he saw the fire. He'd been riding since dawn and figured he should get to Gardiner with time to spare.

Whoever had the fire was off the road, out of sight. He did see two horses tied to an alder tree, and thinking it might be Clayborne and Monroe, he stopped, slid off, and with gun drawn slowly approached. He heard voices.

A few feet away, he stopped. He'd recognized the unmistakable twang of Sarge Hornsby. He yelled, "Sarge, its Jim Albright."

"Over here, Jim. Jesse and I found your deputy. He's still alive."

Crescent Gold

Thirty-Three

Riding to either Gardiner or Sequim and taking the coach had never been an option for Clayborne. Far too risky, he'd told Tressa, so they'd stuck to the trails and less-traveled roads. By his reckoning, if they left camp just after dawn, they would arrive at the trail leading to the south shore around noon.

"Up and at em there sleepy head," he said, giving her a not so gentle poke.

She rolled over and faced him. "Don't call me 'sleepy head', after drinking all of Osgood's flask, your eyes look like two burnt holes in a blanket."

The previous evening they'd camped along the Elwha River. It had been a cold, blustery night and their shelter of hemlock boughs did little to keep out the blowing snow. Neither he nor Tressa had gotten much rest, but it was what they'd heard from a man they'd encountered on the trail that kept Clayborne awake.

"Osgood's bourbon be damned, if I look like hell, it's because I worried all night about what that gent told us – plus my stomach growling and your snoring didn't help."

Crescent Gold

"Worrying about whether there's a hotel built over the spot where you think the treasure is buried isn't going to change anything. Besides you don't know for sure where the exact spot is anyway."

"Yeah, but I feel so stupid, forgot all about that Marymere Hotel being built last year. From what that guy said, the hotel could be smack dab on the spot, or mighty near it."

"C'mon, let's get something to eat," Tressa said. "When we get there, you can get your map out and we'll see, besides, you've got to figure out what that nose thing is."

The stagecoach was ten minutes away from departing Gardiner when the three horses carrying four men rode up to Frank Fisher's small station. Stan had not complained during the ride, but Jim Albright knew he must be hurting. Every time the horse stepped on a rock or into a shallow hole, Stan winced. Twice Albright almost lost his grip trying to keep one arm around his deputy while the other grasped the saddle horn.

During the journey, Albright, Hornsby and Jesse Grayson discussed their options. First priority was to get Stan to the doctor's office, that done, Albright would leave on the stagecoach for Lake Crescent. Sarge, who saw an opportunity for adventure, reluctantly opted out and would get back to Quilcene in order to get needed supplies to the miners in Copper City. That had left it up to Jesse. The lure was way too tempting.

Albright telephoned Sara Munn and she agreed to travel to Port Townsend to be with Honiko. Jesse telephoned Honiko and she urged her husband to stay with his story, and said she would welcome the time with Sara. With that, the Sheriff and the reporter boarded the coach for the journey west.

The clerk at the Marymere was puzzled Ed Nelson didn't have luggage, but when Nelson explained his bags were coming later, paid for his room in full, plus gave him an extra two dollars, he smiled and handed him the room key. Now, five minutes later, Nelson sat in one of the room's red leather chairs and stared out the window.

For the first time since embarking on this quest, he began to have doubts. He had no way to be sure Clayborne would be on the next boat, or any boat for that matter. Clayborne could go any place by horseback. If he did take the boat, would he get off at the Marymere? It also occurred to Nelson that his new persona might not be enough to fool Clayborne when and if he got close enough to shadow him. The hours of practice to rid himself of his Swedish accent would count for something, but he'd had a tough time overcoming his habit of tilting his head when he talked.

He rose and looked in the oval mirror that hung over the bureau. *Will he recognize me?* He glanced at his watch. *Half past eleven.*

From their vantage point on the south side of the lake, Spencer Clayborne and Tressa Monroe watched the side-wheeler ferry pull away. They'd counted five passengers and Clayborne didn't recognize any of them. In his bones he knew

Crescent Gold

Sheriff Albright would be after him – Osgood surely spilled the beans, but for now it looked as if he had some breathing room.

"Let's take another look at the map and then we'd better find a spot to camp for the night," Clayborne said. "It seems like we're in the clear for now."

He once again unrolled his drawing. "As far as I can make out, this spot here," he pointed to the edge of the oblong shape around the heron, "is where the lake is at its narrowest and a likely spot for an Indian village. On an old map I saw at the library, that would be Barnes Point, and guess what, the Marymere hotel sits right on Barnes Point." He looked out over the lake, following the path of the feather. "The problem is, I have nothing to orient distances from."

"What do you mean?"

"The stones are twenty paces each and they lead away from the last feather symbol, see," he pointed again to the map. "They end up at the end of what we think is a nose, but where do they start from – where is the last feather symbol located? Either the Indian village site is where the Marymere now sits, or near it, under the water."

She looked up and wisecracked. "Find a funny nose and a feather. Should be easy."

Thirty-Four

By eleven forty-five, not able to stand the tension any longer, Nelson left his room and walked to the ferry dock. The sky was beginning to cloud over and whitecaps were beginning to form on the lake. He turned up his collar and waited in silence.

Three men and two women disembarked. None of them came close to resembling either Clayborne or Monroe. *Now what? I've either beaten them all here, or I've really messed up.*

After making a supper reservation, Nelson returned to his room.

Pushed by an increasingly strong southerly wind, the light snow that had earlier begun as gently falling flakes was now blowing obliquely. Spencer Clayborne and Tressa Monroe had been following a trail around the lake for two hours, stopping every so often to consult the map. Clayborne was going under the assumption that the feather symbol used on the map had a double meaning. That in general it indicated a measure of distance and direction on Indian drawings, but because in his drawing it was shown near the crossed hands and in line with the "nose" symbol, it indicated a specific starting point.

"Spence, it's getting nasty."

"I know, but let's go on for another few minutes. I just have that gut feeling there's a drawing of a feather somewhere on the shore of the lake, and probably on this side."

She shook her head. "C'mon, we've been looking for hours, even if there was one, either its eroded away, under lots of water or covered by hundreds of years of growth. It could be anywhere and even if it is, you're sure as hell not going to spot it in this light." She stopped. "I'm going back to our camp before I can't find the way." She stared at him. "Frankly, I think we should hightail it out of here while we have the chance and forget this wild goose chase." She stomped her foot. "You coming?"

"All right, but tomorrow I'm going to continue to search, with or without you," Clayborne said. *Bitch!*

The lake ferry pulled away and headed for the Marymere Hotel's dock. The only passengers stood next to the pilot.

"Thanks for making the extra run today, Rudy," Jim Albright said. "Jesse and I really appreciate it."

"My pleasure, Sheriff. Anything for a visiting lawman should put me in good with Sheriff Maxwell."

"Thanks. In case you wondered, your sheriff knows I'm here."

Thirty-Five

Spring 1482

As best Kaiahan could determine, the village lay beneath thirty feet of water, with the communal lodge building nearest to what was now the shoreline.

They'd been at the lake for a day and although the water was ice cold, he and Nootka took turns diving while S'Hai-ak kept the fire going. On his third dive, Nootka reached the top of the longhouse. Kaiahan dove in the same spot and through the crystal clear water, he too saw what had once been the village's communal building.

After several more dives, the men concluded that much of the village lay in shambles at the bottom and unless the lake level lowered considerably they would never be able to recover the bodies of those that were trapped, or salvage anything of value.

However on the second night they discussed if they should dive into the longhouse in an effort to recover some of the golden pendants. Nootka, the youngest of the three, was certain

Crescent Gold

he could make the dive to at least see if he could find the chest they had used to hold the pendants. Kaiahan expressed his concerns about the risk, but both Nootka and S'Hai-ak wanted to try the next morning.

They waved at Nootka as he waded out and dove. When four minutes passed and Nootka had not surfaced, Kaiahan jumped in.

Kaiahan surfaced. "I cannot find him!" he yelled to S'Hai-ak. He dove again, but with the same result.

"I'll try," S'Hai-ak said, wading out.

"No! The water is bitter cold and it is muddy today, hard to see."

"I must try ..."

Kaiahan grabbed the younger man. "No, it is a sign, the Storm God is still angry. We must leave this place, now!"

"But, Nootka ..."

"He is gone." Kaiahan put his hand on the younger man's shoulder. "Come, now ..."

S'Hai-ak hung his head. "Will we ever come back?"

"Perhaps, but not this year. Perhaps never."

Although in his heart Kaiahan felt they would never return, he knew the location of the village buildings and the chest must be more exactly marked should the possibility exist in the future. The general location was shown by the drawing of the shadow cast by their sacred mountain, but he needed a reference point. When they returned to the cave, he could add additional details.

Crescent Gold

Leaving S'Hai-ak to prepare for departure, Kaiahan left their camp site, counting the number of paces as he walked. He looked for a spot to etch a feather, a feather that would mark the starting point.

He was about to give up when he came upon a pile of large rocks, the uppermost jutting out over the water, and as if by fate, its narrow end pointed directly at the sacred mountain's unique shadow, the shadow that lay over the site of the submerged village.

Thirty-Six

December 1907

Breakfast was served at the Marymere Hotel from six to nine. Jesse and the sheriff had agreed to meet in the dining room at six-thirty, but now with the time nearing seven, and his stomach growling embarrassingly loud, he signaled the waiter.

There were other guests when he'd entered the rustically decorated room, a man seated near the large bay window and a young couple two tables from Jesse, next to the log wall. The man by the window had his back to Jesse.

"I'll have coffee now, then scrambled eggs and bacon," Jesse said, pointing to the menu.

"Shall I wait a few more minutes before ordering your eggs and bacon, sir?"

"No, I've waited long enough and he should be here soon." As Jesse spoke he noticed the man at the window all of a sudden turned his head toward him, but just as quickly, turned back.

"I'll be right back with your coffee – ah … cream, sir?"

Crescent Gold

"Yes." He stared at the back of the man's head. *Familiar? Where have I seen him before? In Port Townsend?*

"Sorry I'm late," Albright said, as he entered the dining room and took the chair opposite Jesse.

Jesse could have sworn that the single man's head jerked. "That's all right. I thought you were getting up early."

"I did, but I've been on the telephone to Port Townsend. Larry's doing nicely, by the way."

Jesse didn't respond.

"Did you hear me?"

"I'm sorry." He spoke low to Albright. "See the fellow by the window; does he look familiar to you?"

"I can't see his face, but no, not in particular."

Jesse shrugged his shoulders. "Just my imagination, I guess. I already ordered. I was starved."

He thought he recognized the first voice and caught himself turning to look. *Grayson, the reporter?* There was no mistaking the second voice. *Damn!*

Nelson picked up his cup. *Now what?* He mulled over his options. If his new appearance was any good, he should be able to leave without them recognizing him. If it was not and they recognized him as Sven Olsen, he'd have to make a run for it. *For sure*, he thought, *I'd better keep my mouth shut. Shit, they're at the same hotel!*

He signaled the waiter, and in the lowest voice possible, said, "Check please."

Crescent Gold

The waiter came to Nelson's table, and in so doing blocked anyone's view. "Just sign with your room number sir, which will be fine."

Ed glared at the bill. *Ridiculous*, he thought, *coffee and eggs, one dollar. In Canada eggs are only fifteen cents a dozen.* He quickly scrawled his name and leaving a generous tip of twenty-five cents, rose and hurriedly left the dining room.

There was little doubt Albright was here for the same reason he was, find Clayborne. Equally apparent was Albright hadn't yet found Clayborne. Olsen knew he had to find Clayborne first, all the while keeping a low profile. *But where is the son-of-a-bitch?*

Mindful of Tressa's nasty mood the previous evening, Clayborne lightly shook her. After they'd returned to the campsite, she'd continued to argue for giving up what she now considered a futile search and leaving before they were caught.

"C'mon, we'll have something to eat and start looking again."

She rolled over and faced him. "Good God, Spence, it isn't even light yet."

"By the time we leave it will be. Up and at 'm."

"Up and at 'm yours!"

Thirty minutes later they had returned to the spot where they'd discontinued the search.

"Look," Clayborne said, "The sun's coming out, it's a good sign."

Crescent Gold

Tressa was silent as she followed him along Lake Crescent's southern shore, but she mused that if the morning's search wasn't productive, she would leave. She'd decided that no amount of gold was worth going back to prison.

"Oops – sorry." She'd stumbled into Clayborne who'd abruptly stopped.

"Look!" He gestured toward a cluster of four rocks in a clearing near the edge of the lake. The largest rested near five feet on top of the others and the small end of its diamond-like shape pointed north, toward Storm King Mountain.

"I see, but it's just another odd-shaped bunch of rocks," she said, but he ignored her and hurriedly walked to the formation. "Be careful, Spence, anyone can see you from across the lake."

Ignoring her admonition he walked to the rocks and began searching. "You can help."

Reluctantly she joined him. "You're crazy. If there was some kind of feather mark it would have eroded away or be covered by layers of this moss crap."

"Stop bitching and give me a hand. They're called lichens, by the way, not moss crap. Darn it, Tressa, c'mon, I've got a gut feeling this is the likely spot."

"Go to hell, Spence, a feeling, you have a feeling, Sho…"

He whirled around and grabbed her sleeve, almost pulling off her blue parka. "I mean it! Damn, Tressa, start helping and shut up!"

Silently the two examined the scoured surfaces of the rocks they could reach. Clayborne used his knife to carefully scrape away years of fungal growth, while Tressa, mumbling as she

Crescent Gold

went, pulled away the heavier growths of plant life. Twenty minutes passed, then twenty more.

"I'm going to climb up," Clayborne said, planting one foot in a crevasse and using an outcropping to pull himself up to eye level with the top rock. "Not as much moss up here."

Clayborne used his free hand to scrape, but progress was slow as he frequently had to push the straggly hair from his eyes. A strong breeze had begun to blow in from the west and whitecaps started to form on the lake..

Tressa had worked her way around the base rock and was now exposed to anyone looking across from the Marymere Hotel. "Spencer, this is getting ridiculous, I'm going to be spotted."

He disregarded her and then, "Son of a buck! I think I found it!"

"What, you've got to be kidding," she said, stepping back to look up at him.

What she saw was the unmistakable etching of a feather, its stem pointing in the same direction as the angled surface of the rock and seemingly straight at Barnes Point.

"This has got to be it. Help me down. I want another look at the map."

Thirty-Seven

A movement, ever so slight, caught his eye. He had been staring out his window, trying to decide whether to check out or take his chances that an accidental encounter with the sheriff or Grayson could be risked at the Marymere.

There it was again, a flash of blue. *Someone's by that bunch of rocks across the lake,* he thought, wishing he had binoculars. He strained to see more, raising his line of sight. *Yes!* He spotted another individual climbing down from the top rock. The sun's rays broke from behind the clouds and a gust of wind blew the person's hair. "Clayborne," Nelson said aloud. "Gotcha!"

Wind's picking up," Albright said as they'd left the dining room and sat on down on the cedar plank porch steps. He tried again to light his briar pipe, but the flame was quickly extinguished.

"Maybe it's time to switch to cigarettes, or quit all together," Jesse said. "You, ah ... did you see that?"

"What?"

Crescent Gold

"Over there, I could have sworn I saw somebody climbing on that odd-shaped rock," he said, pointing across the lake. "There, somebody in a blue coat ... now ..."

Albright rose, shielded his eyes and peered in the direction Jesse had indicated. "Don't see anything except the rocks, but the sun's pretty bright."

Jesse kept looking and shook his head. "Whoever or whatever it was, it's gone now ... no, wait, see that, I'm sure that's someone climbing down. See ... darn, oh well."

Holding his face close to the surface of the rock and sighting along the path of the etched feather, Clayborne could see that the symbol pointed in the general direction of the Marymere Hotel. Nothing he saw resembled a nose and without that reference, a more precise location could be anywhere within several hundred yards either side of the hotel.

"Well?" Tressa stood below, hands on hips. "Someone's going to spot you, Spence. Hurry up."

He heeded her warning and jumped down. "I don't get it. This has got to be the marker, but it doesn't really pin anything down. That damn nose thing, I ... shit, I'm missing something." He studied the map again.

"Speaking of 'shit', you've got it for brains. We need to disappear now." She turned and walked away. "It's time to get out of here, head south to Oregon."

"Jeez, Tressa, just let me think a minute, hold up, I know those pendants are around here somewhere, and ...." He reached for her arm, jerking her backwards.

Crescent Gold

Tressa caught her balance and swung at him, hitting him full in the face. "You bastard, let me go, look for your stupid gold, but I'm done."

Clayborne slapped her across the face. "You little bitch." He slapped her again and she stumbled backwards, losing her footing and falling hard to the ground. "Now I'm going to give you what I should have given you … what the …"

The sound of the pistol firing was slightly muffled as Clayborne jumped on her and grabbed for the gun. The gun discharged a second time and the reverberation echoed across the lake.

"Damn you, Tressa, damn!"

When the second shot rang out, Ed Nelson was rounding the edge of the lake, heading in the direction of the rock formation. He was sure it was a gun shot. Nelson hesitated, unsure what to do next. Unarmed and ill-prepared, he knew he didn't want to run pell-mell into Clayborne or Monroe. He listened – no noise, then a thud, thud, the sound of someone running – away from him.

Cautiously he continued.

Nearing the rock formation he heard groaning and could see someone lying on the ground at the base of the rock. Still alert, Nelson walked to the individual and knelt down.

"I'll be damned!"

Nelson had seen enough gunshot wounds to recognize when one was imminently fatal. The groaning had stopped, replaced by a gurgling sound as blood and air mixed.

Crescent Gold

"Looks like it's over for you," Nelson said.

The eyes opened wide. "It's ... ah ... that voice ... I ... how...?"

"How did I get here? Risen from the dead, no, quite alive, Spencer. Yes, it's me, Sven, you old friend the Warrior -- no ghost."

"What, no ... help me ... share gold." He struggled to speak, blood seeping from the corner of his mouth, and Nelson wasn't sure Clayborne really knew to whom he was talking. "Tressa shot me ... treasure, ah ... gold." Clayborne pointed at the rock formation. "Feather, found the feather ... no nose ... damn woman, I ... didn't find nose... lake ...hraaaa ... gaaa."

Nelson felt for a pulse, found none -- Clayborne was dead. *Where the hell's Tressa? Probably her I heard running away.*

He rolled Clayborne over and searched his clothes. Stuffed in one jacket pocket he found a Derringer pistol, in the other he found the map. He started to unroll the map, but stopped. *What's that? Someone's coming, damn!*

Nelson pulled Clayborne's body behind the rocks and dashed into a thick growth of Sitka Spruce and squatted down behind a rotting tree stump, just in time to be missed being seen by Jim and Jesse.

Jim Albright had jumped up from the front porch steps and yelled to Jesse, who'd gone inside to telephone Honiko, when he'd not seen any additional movement across the lake, and tiring of Albright's teasing him about imaginary things.

"Did you hear that? Sure sounded like gunfire."

Crescent Gold

Jesse ran out onto the porch. "Yes, could you tell where from?"

"I'd guess right from where you saw that movement on the rocks. Guess you were right – sorry about the kidding. Let's go see, hurry."

They ran past the dock and turned west up the south side of the lake. Suddenly Albright stopped. "Crap, gun's in my room. Let's slow down just in case. Could have been hunters, I suppose, but let's not take any chances." He started off again. "Keep low."

All of a sudden they entered a clearing near the water and before them stood the large rock formation they'd seen from the Marymere Hotel porch. No one was in sight. Albright walked closer, and then abruptly stopped.

"Look," he said pointing down, "blood."

"Goes over to the rock," Jesse answered.

"Well I'll be damned – Clayborne!" Albright bent down, shaking his head.

"Is he dead?" Jesse asked in hushed tones, as if someone was listening.

"Yup, deader that a doornail," Albright answered, rolling the body over on its stomach. "See, there's the exit wound. Somebody shot him in the gut. What a mess, blew his guts right out of him."

"Do you think it was Tressa Monroe?"

"Could have been, don't know who else. Well for one thing it sure saves Jefferson County a trial." Albright started searching through Clayborne's clothes. "I wonder if he has that map Osgood was talking about."

Crescent Gold

"If it's gone that would mean whoever shot him took it, right?"

Albright didn't answer, but continued his search. He rolled Clayborne's body onto its back. "Nothing here – I guess that would be true Jesse, but if it was Monroe she's got a headstart on us."

"But if she's got the map, wouldn't she stick around and try to find the treasure?"

"Not sure. Right now, I'm not going to worry about her, I need to telephone Sheriff Maxwell, and then we'll take another look round."

She'd climbed into the saddle and headed west.

Tressa had loved Clayborne, but she'd had to make a choice, and she'd chosen freedom. She had a sister in Oregon. Maybe she could start a new life there.

After several hours she was tired and feeling lightheaded, despite having stopped once to rest and have a drink of water. She pushed on to Lake Pleasant.

The road around the lake was full of ruts and exposed rocks and Tressa winced as the horse stumbled. Looking at her leg she saw that the rag she'd used as a bandage was turning a bright crimson.

Thirty-Eight

Autumn

Kaiahan watched admiringly as his son suckled noisily at O'Wota's breast. He gently brushed back the hair from his mate's eyes and rose from their bed.

"It is cold for this time of the season. I will put some wood on the coals."

"Your son is hungry this morning, Kaiahan."

He smiled. "He is hungry all the time. He will grow taller than his father."

When S'Hai-ak and Kaiahan had returned from the lake they convinced the elders that, at least for the foreseeable future, returning to the site of their former winter home and rebuilding was out of the question. On their return trip to the cave they

Crescent Gold

had taken an easterly route along the water, seeking a favorable location for a new winter village.

On their second day of travel, about twenty miles from the great lake they found what seemed to be an ideal spot. Near the water, the area was shielded by a long hook of land. The tribe could easily reach the sea, but the harbor and village would be protected from storms by a natural barrier. Kaiahan would later argue that the site could be their permanent home – a home for all seasons. He believed their artisans could make a yearly trip to the cave, harvest the gold and craft the pendants. It would not be necessary for the tribe to make the semi-annual trek.

There would be a meeting of the full tribe in two days. If they were to move to the new location in time to construct new lodges, they would need to depart soon.

Kaiahan had even suggested a name for their new village, Tse-whit-zen, which meant, new beginnings.

They had begun immediately to construct temporary lodges using the abundant supply of cedar bark, ferns and salal; now a month later the tribe was building what would be their permanent homes.

At the edge of the bay stood a massive stand of Cedar trees and these were providing more than enough material for multi-family lodges and a communal longhouse. Also a discovery by Kaiahan and S'Hai-ak aided the tribe in the erection of the village. As the men had removed the thick ground vegetation they had uncovered the remnants of several structures. These had proved to be rock solid and very suitable for building upon.

Crescent Gold

By early autumn six cedar plank lodges were nearing completion. Planks up to three feet wide and from four to six inches thick had been cut by means of wedges made of elk's horn or flint. Using these planks and logs, rectangular lodges up to 100 feet or more in length and fifteen to twenty feet wide would be ready for the winter season.

This day, Kaiahan had risen early and walked with O'Wota to the creek. Their child was wrapped in deer fur and bound to a wooden cradleboard strapped to her back.

"Our lodge will soon be finished." He reached down and took the leather-lined vessel. "Here, let me carry that."

O'Wota smiled at her mate. "You have worked hard, Kaiahan." She stopped. "Do you ever wonder about the people who were here before us?"

"Yes. The elders believe they may have been our ancestors, the ancient people."

"I wonder why they left this spot, it is so beautiful."

"Beautiful like you," he said, setting down the water vessel and pulling her to himself.

"But the baby …?"

"He can continue sleeping on the ground – our son needs a brother."

O'Wota boldly grinned and unstrapped the cradleboard, "Perhaps a sister."

Thirty-Nine

Jesse and Jim watched as the ferry carrying Clallam County Sheriff Ben Maxwell and the body of Spencer Clayborne pulled away.

"Well, that's that, I guess," Jim Albright said, turning away from the Marymere Hotel's dock.

"How about Tressa Monroe, aren't you going to search for her?"

"We followed that trail of blood from the rock to the campsite, but there it stopped. I imagine she took one of the horses. Where she went, who knows? I telephoned the sheriffs in all the local counties and Sheriff Maxwell will put out bulletins when he gets back to town. It's about all I can do; it's out of my jurisdiction."

"You're right. Might as well call my editor with what I've got and check out of the hotel."

"I've got a better idea," Albright said, mounting the steps to the hotel entrance. "Do you know what day it is?"

"Ah … yes, it's December 23rd."

Crescent Gold

"And -- which means?" Albright raised his hands, shoulder high, and palms open.

"It's two days before Christmas," Jesse answered, nodding.

"That's right and I think we both deserve a break. I checked with the hotel and they have ours and another room available through the twenty-sixth. How about we telephone Port Townsend and have the ladies join us?"

Jesse smiled broadly. "Great idea ... hey, I thought the hotel was booked solid."

"It was, seems one guest unexpectedly checked out at noon today."

Ed Nelson had the map spread out on his bed at the Log Cabin Hotel. His accommodations were more rustic than his room at the Marymere, but it had the prime advantage of being across the lake from where the sheriff was lodged, and equally important for his plans, on a road that led to Port Crescent and the Strait of Juan de Fuca.

So far he'd surmised that the site of the cache of gold pendants was very likely under water, probably near the Marymere. From Clayborne's dying ramblings he knew the rock formation held some of the secrets to pinning down a more exact location. He'd have to return to that spot soon.

Clayborne had mentioned a "feather" several times and Nelson believed the feathers on the map signified direction and probably distance. He also figured the stone symbols indicated distance. The symbol that eluded interpretation was the one that looked like a person's nose.

Crescent Gold

Nelson checked his watch. Ten before noon. Rolling up the map, he left his room and walked to the dock, where the small rowboat he'd rented for the day was tied to a piling.

He glanced to the west. "Blue sky and no wind, should be an easy crossing," he said out loud, and for the first time in awhile, not trying to camouflage his Swedish accent.

Nelson had rowed for a landing spot on the south shore that looked to be about a hundred feet west of the rock formation. Now safely ashore, he experienced a sense of elation as he stood in front of the rock.

When he'd seen Clayborne from across the lake, his old nemesis had been climbing on the upper rock, the one with the long diamond shape. He removed the map from his pocket. *Now, what have I missed? The feather.*

Careful not to expose himself any more than necessary to someone looking from the Marymere, he found a toe hold and pulled himself up. And there it was, the symbol of a feather etched into the rock, and its end pointed toward the Marymere Hotel. He'd found the "mark", but he thought to himself, *Now what?* He started to descend.

Then he saw it. The distinctive shadow cast by the sun shining behind Storm King Mountain – the shadow of a nose. Actually, it looked more like a right triangle except for the indentation at the bottom, giving the effect of a nostril. The line representing the bridge of "nose" was flat with a slight curve at the end. He could see why the ancient artist drew the shadow like it was, and why Clayborne thought it was a drawing of a nose.

Crescent Gold

Sighting again along the direction of the etched feather he saw that his line of sight intersected the end of the nose. It was as if someone had drawn two lines on top of the lake, one along the bridge of the "nose", the other an imaginary line from the rock. The lines intersected in the lake, forming an X. The "X" was not out in the deeper water, but just off shore to the left of the Marymere Hotel.

Nelson tried to remember something he'd heard. *What was it?* It nagged at him.

He climbed down, racking his memory as he went. Then it came to him. A tavern was to be built on Barnes Point on property next to the Marymere Hotel. "Fee Fann!" he swore in his native tongue.

Chapter Forty

The fog that had settled over Lake Crescent began to lift and a toot of its horn signaled the *Storm King* was leaving the dock and heading toward Barnes Point. Jesse and Jim walked down the path from the Marymere Hotel. They continued the conversation they'd had over lunch.

"I still think we ought to look around that rock some more," Jesse said. "Clayborne must have been there for a reason."

"We can, but without any map we'd be shooting in the dark. You're right, though, there's plenty of reason to believe Clayborne discovered the location of the treasure – probably why he and Tressa fought."

"So maybe we can find it."

"Could be, but I still think it'd be a wild goose chase. Besides, whatever is there has been hidden or lost for a long time, maybe it's best left alone – might disturb sacred ground and we'd have that old Indian gent over in La Poel after us ."

"Maybe … oh, here they come."

The side-wheel ferry pulled close to the dock and Rudy threw a rope to Jim Albright who stood next to a smiling Jesse Grayson.

Crescent Gold

"Catch," the pilot said. Then he motioned to his two passengers. "I believe these young ladies are here to see the two of you."

"You bet they are, Rudy," Albright answered, as he made fast the line and offered his hand to Sara Munn.

Garlands of cedar boughs tied in red ribbons hung everywhere and a large wreath adorned the dining room fireplace. Candles on a freshly cut fir tree burned brightly, adding to the festive aura of the room. A nattily attired young waiter filled their water glasses and handed them menus encased in red leather folders.

"Our special tonight in honor of the holiday is turkey with all the trimmings, followed by a choice of pumpkin or mincemeat pie and coffee. I'll be back to get your orders."

"Perhaps the turkey is from your farm," Honiko said, looking at Sara.

"Could be, we sell them all over Washington."

"Before we order, Jesse and I want to tell you both about some ideas we have for the next two days," Jim said, setting down his menu.

Sara winked at Jesse. "Oh, well I can guess one."

"No, no, something else," Jesse said, blushing.

Jim ignored the repartee and continued. "First thing in the morning we'd like to take a hike to Marymere Falls. It's supposed to be spectacular, especially this time of year. It's less than a mile from here. Then tomorrow night we've arranged for a special Christmas Eve dinner. On Christmas day

Crescent Gold

we're going to take a buggy ride to Piedmont and have lunch at the Log Cabin Hotel."

"Sounds great, you two," Sara said. She looked at Honiko. "What do you think?"

Honiko nodded. "Yes, it is fine. It will be hard to leave for San Francisco."

Ed Nelson ate alone in his room at the Log Cabin Hotel. He'd been tempted to join the revelers in the dining room, but had more important things on his mind than singing a bunch of Christmas carols and acting jolly. He was, however, in a ho-ho-ho mood.

He was very cheerful in fact, in high spirits because he had a solution to his problem – how to recover any treasure that most certainly was in Lake Crescent. The way out of his dilemma lay on the nightstand by his bed.

The pamphlet heading was in bold type – WANTED – EXPERIENCED WORKERS – **SINGER'S LAKE CRESCENT TAVERN** CONTRUCTION – APPLY TO …

Crescent Gold

Part Three

Crescent Gold

Marymere Hotel

Forty-One

1908

The body of Tressa Monroe had been found by two men from Beaver. They'd been deer hunting near Lake Pleasant and came upon her frozen remains. They told their friends that, no pun intended, "it was not a pleasant sight."

Clallam County Sheriff Ben Maxwell had telephoned Jim Albright and asked him to attend the Coroner's inquest that would be held at the courthouse in Port Angeles in a week. Jim recalled part of the conversation.

"What about Clayborne?" Jim had asked. "You've never had an inquest for him, and he's been dead for a couple months."

"The Coroner's going to do them both the same day – Clayborne's been on ice in the morgue. Call it a Clallam County Corpse special – two for the price of one. So you see, you have to come."

"Funny Ben, very funny – ha ha," Jim had said.

Crescent Gold

The timing couldn't have been worse as he and Sara were planning to announce their engagement the same week, but in the final analysis, he'd agreed to attend. The announcement could wait a week.

Jim telephoned Jesse at the *Chronicle* the next day to give him the details, only to learn he was at the hospital with Honiko and their new daughter. He reached him later at home and congratulated the new father.

Today Jim was packing for the trip to Port Angeles. The inquest would mark the end of a saga that had begun almost two years before when he traveled to the Tubal Cain mine in the Buckhorn Wilderness of the Olympic Mountains.

In the same courthouse where the inquest would be held, but one day earlier, a judge would rule on the injunction filed by the S'Klallam Tribe. Simply stated the tribe wished to stop the excavation of the land, and the subsequent construction of Avery Singer's tavern on Barnes Point at Lake Crescent. Their claim, the land was sacred, being the site of an ancient S'Klallam village that contained the remains of their ancestors.

The lawyers for the Singer family and Wyle Construction Company had argued there was no proof to the Indian's claim. The attorneys for the S'Klallam claimed that Chetzemoka, a tribal historian and son of a former chief who lived in La Poel, had knowledge that would prove the claim; however the proof turned out to be what the judge had called "lore" and not admissible proof.

Ed Nelson knew his chances of finding the cache of gold pendants depended on being involved with the excavation and

Crescent Gold

construction of the tavern. His experience had been noted by Wyle Construction and as such, Ed had been elevated to the position of foreman, giving him unsupervised access to the site. On the other hand if excavation was halted there wouldn't be any people about, but he knew by himself he stood little chance of finding the cache. And there was something else. Before excavation had been halted, Ed had become more convinced the cache of gold was under water. That fact guaranteed he'd need help, underwater help.

The Singer's wanted a dock for the tavern which would mean driving pilings in the lake and divers would be needed at the onset of the project. Divers were what Ed needed.

He especially needed one diver who was greedy. Three divers had answered the advertisement in the *Port Angeles Evening News* and George Wyle asked Ed to interview the candidates.

The interviews were scheduled the next day. One diver's name, Rex Thornton, was familiar to Ed, but so far he had not been able to remember where he'd heard it.

As Ed made his way to the courthouse, he mused about the gang he used to have at Tubal-Cain and silently wished he had a few of them with him now. Besides a diver, he needed another cohort, and he'd been grooming one for several weeks. His previous personification, The Warrior, was readying to do battle.

Despite a last minute, impassioned appeal by the attorney for S'Klallam Nation, the judge ruled against their injunction, allowing Wyle Construction to carry on excavation for the new

Crescent Gold

Singer's Lake Crescent Tavern. George Wyle, his administrative secretary Lily Ellis and Ed Nelson smiled broadly and thanked their attorneys. Wyle and Lily Ellis would return immediately to Lake Crescent to get the crew back to work while Ed would remain in Port Angeles to conduct the interviews for divers.

The minute Ed saw Rex Thornton he remembered. It was a night in Port Townsend, over a year ago.

When he'd heard the talk about gold pendants being smuggled through Port Townsend, he had always suspected Spencer Clayborne but never had proof of his duplicity. Later when it became clear that the origin of the pendants was from the Buckhorn Wilderness of the Olympic Mountains, he was even more convinced of Clayborne's involvement and when Ed was doing some mine company business in Port Townsend and spotted Clayborne one night, he followed him.

Clayborne met a man in a tavern and that man was Rex Thornton. The trip to Port Townsend didn't turn up anything to prove participation in the pendant smuggling, but now, a year later, Ed knew of Clayborne's ultimate guilt and the fact that he'd met with Thornton was very timely knowledge. If Thornton had dealt with Clayborne, *well*, Ed thought, *two plus two equals four.*

Forty-Two

Jim Albright was impressed with the Clallam County Coroner's efficiency. The inquest was over in twenty minutes, the rulings: Spencer Clayborne – death by gunshot wound to the heart, likely shot by Tressa Monroe; Tressa Monroe -- death by exposure and subsequent loss of blood caused by gunshot wound to the thigh, evidence pointed to Spencer Clayborne as the shooter.

"Well, that's over with," said Sheriff Ben Maxwell as he and Jim left the courthouse.

"Yeah, hardly worth the trip, but I'm glad I came, it does close the book on the whole sad tale."

"How about a beer?" Maxwell asked. "The Dupuis Tavern is just a few blocks away, and if you can stay for dinner, they serve up a mean Dungeness crab dinner."

"A beer would taste great, and I've heard about their crab, so yes, and I'm starved. I think I'll stay the night anyway and head back tomorrow."

Ben, you see that guy over by the lamp – no, to your right."

Crescent Gold

Maxwell stared for a moment. "Yeah, that's the new foreman for Wyle Construction. He was here for the injunction hearing on Singer's Tavern up at Lake Crescent. My deputy said he's been interviewing for divers today, now that things went Wyle's way."

"Who's the other man"? Jim asked.

"I haven't seen him around before, maybe someone else with Wyle. Don't know too many of their people." He turned back to face Jim. "Do you believe you know the foreman? I think his name is Nelson," Ben said. "Yeah, Ed Nelson, hear he's from Canada originally."

"Doesn't ring a bell, but damn, I've seen him before, somewhere ... ah, yes, I think that's the guy Jesse recognized when we were at the Marymere in December, and you know, I'm sure I've seen him in Port Townsend ... hmm ... there's something about the way he holds his head."

"Probably there on business," Maxwell said. "They're always coming across."

Jim took a sip of his beer. "Nelson, you say, that does sound familiar. No ..."

"Maybe he used to work at the mill; a lot of those Canucks have worked there."

"Hmm ... could be, but ... ah here's our crab, I'm starved," Jim said as the waiter approached. "You're probably right, Port Townsend gets lots of traffic – let's eat."

"You do remember how to attack these baby's don't you?" Maxwell asked, picking a shell cracker.

"Yes I do, but I haven't had Dungeness crab for quite a while, so this is a real treat."

Crescent Gold

"Those guys at that table over there have been staring at us," Rex Thornton said to Ed.

Ed didn't turn around. "Do you know them?"

"The one with his back to you is Ben Maxwell, the local sheriff, the other looks familiar, but I don't think so."

"Probably just curious – lawmen can be that way. I'll have a peek when I get a chance. Now, let's get back to business." Ed sounded calm, but deep down he was disturbed that the county sheriff and whoever was with him was apparently giving them the once over. He kept his voice as low as possible and continued.

"Sounds like you've got the experience we need, now," he paused for effect – "tell me about Spencer Clayborne."

Thornton's sudden hand jerk knocked his beer glass. "What the …hell …"

"Relax," Ed reached across and grabbed the toppling glass. "You knew Clayborne; I know that, just what kind of dealings did you two have together?"

"What the crap does that have to do with hiring me as a diver for Wyle?" Thornton pushed back his chair as if to leave the table, his face turning red. "This is …"

"Everything. Now simmer down Rex, we don't want those curious fellows looking our way again, do we?" Ed looked sternly at Thornton, almost threatening, then – a broad smile.

"Who the hell are you?" Thornton asked.

"Someone who can make you wealthy, if you're as smart as I think you are and someone who doesn't mind breaking a law or two to get what he wants." Ed paused – "Now, what about Clayborne?"

Crescent Gold

Thornton took a deep breath, looked Nelson in the eyes and decided they may just be "birds of a feather". His thin lips formed a sly smile and he relaxed in his chair.

"He and Vince Menucci hired me to take some packages to a ship in Port Townsend."

"A ship? Why you, I mean anybody could take …"

Rex leaned across the table. "The ship wasn't in port. It would anchor in the harbor near Indian Island and I'd take my dingy from Union Wharf to go out there."

"How often?"

"About once every two weeks and always at night."

"But, why you?" Ed asked, repeating himself. "Lots of men have boats tied up at Union Wharf. They certainly didn't need a diver to row a dingy."

"Vince Menucci and I did some time together in the pokey at Fort Warden back in '02. I sort of owed him a favor."

"So you knew what he was doing was illegal?"

"I guessed it might be, but the diving business was slow and I needed the money, and as I said, I owed him one."

"You had to have been curious -- ever look in the packages?"

Rex hesitated, and gave a slight nod. "Once – that's when my price went up, but a month later it was all over. Heard Menucci was dead and Clayborne in jail."

Ed nodded. "Yup, was in jail, now long dead."

"Now it's your turn," Rex uttered, his regained confidence obvious in the tone of his voice.

Crescent Gold

"Clayborne and I had a relationship at the Tubal-Cain mine – it's a long story, but I bet what you saw in that package at Union Wharf glistened like gold."

Union Wharf – Port Townsend, circa 1908

Forty-Three

Larry had the information Jim had telephoned about on his desk when he returned to the office in Port Townsend, and now sat patiently as his boss scanned the contents of the folder.

"I knew that name was familiar," Jim said, looking up at his deputy. "It's such a common name, I wasn't sure."

"Yup'" Larry said proudly, "I kinda thought it was too, and when you asked me to check back at least two years, I thought you were going daffy, but there it is."

"So an Ed Nelson was staying in town the day before Clayborne's trial last year and somebody with the same name was one of the three men that drew out large sums of money two years ago when we were searching for Sven Olsen, and even more interesting, it looks like the same Ed Nelson took the Pacific Coast Ferry to Victoria the next day," Jim concluded.

"The very same day we thought Sven was leaving on the *Enterprise*." Larry added. "It could be just coincidence, as you said, the name's pretty common and two years…"

Crescent Gold

Jim interrupted. "Did the manifest for the ferry in '06 show Nelson as a US citizen?"

"I can't remember, but I'll have another look at Pacific's records. Why, what are you driving at?"

"Too farfetched to tell you now, but I've got a couple leads to follow; made a couple phone calls, probably just my imagination working overtime. Now, about the other man Nelson was with."

"From your description it could only be one guy, Rex Thornton. He's a local deep sea diver, and he's about the age you figured, balding, about five-five to five-six, but the real clincher, Rex Thornton has a scar on his left cheek." Larry continued, "Now here's something else, Thornton did time a couple years ago for petty theft."

"Hmm, that is interesting. Where'd he do time?"

"Right here at Fort Warden. I've got a telephone call into them now to see what else I can turn up. I should hear back soon."

Albright stood up. "Great work, Larry. This all may mean nothing, but I've got this gut feeling."

The telephone rang and Larry walked to the outer office to answer. "It's a guy with Pacific Coast Steamship calling from Victoria," he hollered to Jim. "He says he's returning your telephone call."

Jim took the earpiece from Larry, leaned forward and spoke into the bell-shaped mouthpiece of the wall-mounted telephone. "Sheriff Albright." For a few minutes he said nothing, just listened. Then, "The *Valencia*, well I'll be damned. Thanks, I appreciate it."

Crescent Gold

Jim replaced the earpiece in its cradle and turned toward Larry. "It turns out our Mr. Nelson was one of the survivors of the *Valencia* sinking."

The telephone call from Fort Warden came the next morning while Jim was having breakfast with Sara at her hotel. Larry was beside himself – Jim would, in his words, "bust a gut" when he heard.

Forty-Four

Excavation was in full swing when Ed returned to Lake Crescent and next to the portable saw mill stood enough timber to start laying the foundation for Singer's Tavern. He found Lily Ellis and George Wyle in the hastily-built cabin which served as the project office. The smoky brown Labrador Retriever lying next to Lily looked up, wagged his tail and nestled his head back in-between his paws. The dog had shown up at the cabin the previous week and was now a permanent fixture at the job site, especially as Lily fed him every day and when it was cold, allowed the Lab to stay in the cabin.

"So, we have a new addition. What's her name?"

"His name is Lucky," Lily answered.

Ed walked over to the dog and scratched him behind the ears. "Good boy, Lucky, glad to see me, huh."

The dog didn't wag his tail this time.

Wyle pointed at the dog. "Lucky's hiding in here, all the noise outside this morning spooked the old guy."

Crescent Gold

"Yeah, looks like you didn't waste any time getting the crew back to work," Ed said.

"Nope, how'd you do in Port Angeles?" Wyle asked, slipping his large bulk off the stool.

"Great, hired Rex Thornton as our diver. Good experience and available. He'll be here tomorrow. I thought we should get going on the dock right away."

"It sounds good to me, Ed. I'm leaving for Forks in an hour to attend my high school reunion, should be back by Friday. You've got all the drawings and between you and Lily I don't think you'll need me for a while. If that Indian bunch from La Poel tries any more shenanigans, telephone Sheriff Maxwell. I don't think they will, though." Wyle nodded at Lily and walked out the door. The Lab rose, as if to follow, but walked to Lily and plopped down.

"You're a sight for sore eyes – here," Ed said. He reached into his jacket pocket and removed a small box tied with a blue ribbon. "Here, this is for you."

Lily hurriedly untied the ribbon and removed the ld. "Ed! It's beautiful, but I can't accept it, it's …"

"It's just my way of saying I missed you and hoping for a lasting friendship, and, ah … you know how I feel about you." He bowed slightly.

She held the cameo brooch up to the sunlight coming through the window. "Well …"

A small smile appeared on her face, a countenance with telltale wrinkles surrounded by strands of graying hair. Lily Ellis at forty-one had worked diligently and purposefully to attain her position at Wyle Construction, a job normally held by a man. She had grown up in Port Angeles, the youngest of four children and although she'd had two romantic relationships in her twenty's, marriage had never been offered, and now her job as George Wyle's assistant was her life. That was until Ed Nelson appeared.

Ed seemed not to mind that her once hourglass figure had morphed into a two-hour glass. In fact he had commented more than once that he loved a full-figured woman. Their romance had thus far not gone beyond a few hurried kisses, but Lily was anticipating and eager for their relationship to expand, and the gift she now held in her hands seemed to signify her wishes were being fulfilled.

"I love it," she said, raising her head and pursing her lips.

He bent down and kissed her quivering lips. "We'd better be careful," he said, quickly straightening up and glancing out the window. "How about we meet after supper?"

She smiled. "Yes. I'll put on a dress for you. These old pants can't be very becoming."

"You look great in anything. Now about tomorrow, this fellow Rex Thornton will be here on the first boat and I want him to begin immediately to search the area off shore for the best spots to sink the dock pilings. I'll have to work directly with him for a while, so you'll have to handle the rest of the crew."

Lily beamed. "Why, yes, I can do that and if I do need any help …"

He leaned in again and gave her a peck on the lips. "You'll know where to find me." *It's so easy,* he mused, *like putty in my hands.* "Till later then."

Crescent Gold

Ed left the job shack and walked toward his crew that was busily clearing away some newly fallen cedar trees. Tomorrow could come none too soon, he thought, but tonight he'd have to play the passionate lover once again.

Crescent Gold

Forty-Five

Sara Munn looked across the table at her soon-to-be announced fiancé. "So, it's all over, the whole Clayborne thing?"

"Yes, over and done with as far as Spencer Clayborne and Tressa Monroe."

"What about the lawyer, Taylor Osgood?"

"I think he'll get a light sentence, unless our fine Judge Fleming is in one of his foul moods." He hesitated and reached across to take her hand. "There is one thing that keeps nagging at me, but nothing that should interfere with our plans, if that's what's bothering you."

"No – I was just curious. What's the 'nagging' thing?" Sara asked.

"Well, there's this guy Nelson that's the new foreman for Wyle over at Lake Crescent, and there's something familiar about him that, I don't know … ah … and several odd coincidences going back two years …"

"What?" she squeezed his hand and smiled. "Don't worry, it will come to you. Now, let's talk about our wedding before you jump up and say you're late for work."

Crescent Gold

"Maybe we should go up to your room where it's quiet?" Jim grinned.

You're late," Larry cried out as soon as Jim entered the office.

"Give a guy a break, besides, who's the boss around here – only kidding. What's the big deal, I can see you've got ants in your pants over something."

"Guess who Rex Thornton's cellmate was over at Fort Warden prison?" his deputy exclaimed.

"I … ah …"

"Vince Menucci!" Larry blurted out, not giving Jim a chance to answer.

"I'll be dipped. Menucci, now that's interesting." *And I just told Sara that the Clayborne fiasco was a dead subject*, he thought. "Well, that only proves that Thornton knew Menucci… um…Menucci, Clayborne."

"So you don't think there's anything crooked going on?" Larry asked, sounding disappointed.

"No, he served his time, but, you know it does seem a bit weird, almost too coincidental. We've got this Nelson fellow, who we found out was a *Valencia* survivor who drew out a large sum of money before he took the ferry to Victoria a year ago, at the same time we were looking for Clayborne and Sven Olsen. Then we have Nelson coming back here about the same time as Clayborne's trial and escape – now he's working for Wyle where he's interviewing Thornton who knew Clayborne's cohort Menucci." Jim paused and furrowed his brow as if trying to remember something else. "Hmm – even more interesting is that Lake Crescent seems to be at the center

Crescent Gold

of it all. That's where Clayborne went to find some mystical treasure, Nelson was there at the Marymere Hotel and now he's back there and probably working with Thornton."

"You never found the map that Osgood told you about, did you?"

"No I didn't, and whatever came of it, or if it was really a map to a treasure died with Clayborne and Monroe. Besides, that's Sheriff Maxwell's jurisdiction."

"So you're going to consider the whole shebang closed," Larry said. "You know, there may be some truth to a treasure hidden at Lake Crescent – aren't you at least curious?"

"Maybe a little, but without the so-called map, and Clayborne and Monroe gone, it's just a good story. Too bad Jesse's not still here to write it. I can just imagine his title – The Crescent Lake Gold Mystery."

Larry nodded and hunched his shoulders. "All right, I guess that's it."

"Yup. I'll phone Ben Maxwell tomorrow and run the whole mess by him, but for us here in Jefferson County, as you said, that's about it."

"Oh, that reminds me, this registered letter came for you late yesterday. I signed for it," Larry said. "It's from the U.S. Marshal's office in Olympia."

Jim opened the letter. "Well, I'll be damned, I've been appointed Deputy U.S. Marshal for this district.

"No kidding. Did you know about it?"

"In a way, Ben Maxwell submitted my name last month, but frankly, I'd forgotten all about it with all the Clayborne mess going on."

Crescent Gold

"When's it effective?"

"Says here all I have to do to accept is telephone Olympia and then get sworn in," Jim answered. "The local federal judge can do the swearing in."

Forty-Six

1485

Earthquakes had occurred occasionally during Kaiahan's lifetime, but he was convinced the one that woke him the morning of his son Patkanim's third birthday had been stronger than the one that had destroyed their former home on the great lake. Their new village of Tse-whit-zen had come out of the recent quake with minimal damage.

The senior elder claimed he had a vision that the village had risen from the sea – that the quake was a good omen foretelling the coming of great wealth to the S'Klallam people. As a result of his vision, the elders asked Kaiahan and S'Hai-ak to return to the site of Tien-ah in hopes they might recover the box that held the gold pendants.

It had been wishful thinking in Kaiahan's mind so he was as shocked as S'Hai-ak when, after two days travel, they crested the hill and looked down. Visible above the water was the cedar bark roof of the longhouse. Why the lake level had lowered, whether it would rise again or how quickly, Kaiahan couldn't comprehend, but he somehow knew that if they had any chance at recovery, they needed to act now.

Crescent Gold

S'Hai-ak made the first dive. Remembering what had happened before; Kaiahan was starting to get worried when S'Hai-ak broke the surface.

"I found the box, but I can't lift it," he said, gasping for breath.

"Did you try to remove the top?"

"It wouldn't open," S'Hai-ak said as pulled himself through the hole and onto the roof.

"Rest a moment longer and I'll dive with you."

Kaiahan waded out and jumped into the clear, blue lake and swam to the rooftop.

S'Hai-ak dove through the opening in the roof of the longhouse and disappeared. Kaiahan followed, but once he passed through the opening he found himself in darkness and began to panic until he felt S'Hai-ak's strong grip. Slowly his eyes adjusted to the half-light.

They swam deeper and Kaiahan recognized they were entering the council room of the elders, the room where the box containing the pendants had been stored. He spotted the box where S'Hai-ak had left it.

Each taking a side, the two friends pushed away from the floor and with what air and energy remained, kicked upwards toward the light.

They broke the surface, both panting for breath. "We have it," said S'Hai-ak. "The elders will be greatly pleased."

"Yes, but we must make sure this box contains the pendants."

"It must," answered S'Hai-ak, "it was in the elder's chambers and it is heavy – heavy with the yellow metal, surely the great Storm God has favored us with this treasure."

Forty-Seven

The ferry arrived on schedule at the Marymere Hotel dock. Its only passenger was Rex Thornton. Ed was waiting at the end of the dock.

"We'll need some help with the gear," Rex said, "especially the air cylinders, they weigh a ton."

"You don't use a pump anymore?" Ed asked.

"Some divers still do, but I've been using this newer way. I bought the outfit last year from an ex-navy diver. Strap the air cylinder's to my back and the air line connects to my helmet. You'll see."

As they made their way up the ramp, Ed spotted Lily running toward them. "Here comes the gal I was telling you about – she looks shook up about something."

"Ed, Ed, we may have a big hitch!"

"C'mon, it can't be that bad." He turned to Rex. "Lily, this is our diver, Rex Thornton. Rex, Lily."

"A pleasure," Lily said, "but Ed, I'm serious. That crazy Indian was here a while ago yelling at the crew. He said he'd be back tomorrow and for us to stay out of the lake."

Crescent Gold

"Don't worry, he's all talk and no action, besides, we've got the sheriff on our side and if the old coot causes any trouble, we'll call the law. C'mon Rex it's time to earn your keep."

The crew watched in awe as Rex donned his rubberized suit, strapped on two air tanks and with Ed's help, put on the helmet and attached the lines. Rex looked like an alien monster that they'd seen pictures of in science fiction comic books. The only thing missing was the ray gun.

"All right you guys, back to work," Ed hollered to his men, as Rex waded into the lake. "Show's over."

Earlier Ed had sent Lily on an errand so he and Rex could go over Clayborne's map and Ed's observations from the rock with the feather etching.

When he first showed the map to Rex in Port Angeles, Rex had been skeptical, but when Ed told him that very likely a stash of gold pendants like he'd seen in Clayborne's package was at the bottom of the lake, Rex signed on. They would split the booty sixty percent for Ed, forty for Rex.

The precise location of the pendants was, of course, still a matter of conjecture, but Ed was sure that the spot indicated on the map by the crossed hands and heron was the location of an ancient Indian dwelling or several dwellings – possibly a village, and where the nose shadow crossed the line of sight from the rock lay the exact location. They'd know more after the first dive.

Standing alone at the edge of the lake, Ed checked his Waltham pocketwatch. *He's been down almost fifteen minutes*, he thought. Just when he began to be concerned, up popped the

Crescent Gold

helmet and a few strokes later Rex was standing in shallow water.

"Mostly a big pile of timbers, but I think you're right, it probably was a good-sized village. There's one larger building still mostly intact, but I need to take a breather."

"So you can see well enough?"

"Yeah, I'm using an underwater flare, they don't last long, but they give me pretty good visibility. Besides, it's only about thirty feet to the bottom, so there's some natural light getting through."

"What's next?" Ed asked.

"If I can find an opening that looks safe, I'll go inside the large building and have a look around." He hesitated. "You know, the floor of the lake has years of sediment. If those pendants are lying on the bottom, there's no way I'll find them."

"I know, but I figure they probably kept them in some kind of container, not loose, and if that large building was their communal longhouse, that's probably where they were stowed."

"Okay, give me a hand tightening the backpack straps and lifting the helmet into place, there isn't a lot of daylight left," Rex said.

Fifteen minutes later Rex resurfaced.

"I got into the building and explored about half way. It's in amazing good shape – almost undamaged except for a gaping hole in the top that I went through."

"Did you see anything that looks like it could hold the pendants?"

Crescent Gold

"Nope, but I was losing my torch light and had to get out. We'll have to continue tomorrow."

"All right. Now remember, if anyone asks, you're looking for good spots to drive in pilings for the dock," Ed said. "C'mon, get dried off. Supper's in an hour."

Wyle Construction leased two of the Marymere Hotel's cabins. One was occupied by George Wyle. As foreman, Ed Nelson had been given the use of the second, and for the next several nights he would be sharing it with Rex.

When Wyle was traveling to other job sites, Lily often used his cabin overnight, rather than travel the dark road to her home in Piedmont. Lily heard the three knocks at the door.

"Come in," she said softly, knowing full well who it was.

Clad in a flower print bathrobe, Lily was seated in a wicker chair next to the four poster bed. A tea pot and two cups were on the nightstand and Lucky lay curled up at her feet.

"You look lovely tonight, my dear, but how about we let Lucky out for a while?"

"All right, Ed. Why don't you pour the tea while I do that."

As she rose the robe parted revealing an ample bosom. She caught Ed's eye. "Naughty, naughty, no peeks."

Before taking off his coat, Ed removed a small flask and poured some of the contents in each cup. "There that should add a little zip."

"Some of my favorite elixir, I assume," she said closing the door and coming up behind him.

Crescent Gold

Ed turned and pulled at the robe's cloth tie. "You bet, now let's see what you're hiding." He stood back as the robe parted. "Oh my. How absolutely delectable."

She moaned as his hands explored, at first gently kneading and then as her breathing became heavy, more intensely. "The … tea can wait, I think … oh …?"

Forty-Eight

Ed and Rex were finishing breakfast in the large tent George Wyle had set up as a food kitchen for the employees when Lily came running in, followed by Lucky.

"Ed, you won't believe it – we've got a really big problem now."

"Oh Lily, nothing's that big of a problem." He reached down and gave Lucky a pat. The dog growled softly. "What's going on?"

"You'll have to see for yourself. Follow me."

Both men rose and followed, and only got a few feet out the tent door when they saw the crew clustered near the lake's edge. Ed took several long strides and reached the men.

"Son of a bitch!" Ed mumbled as he pushed through workers lining the shore. "What the hell! Damn, there must be a couple dozen of them."

"Twenty by my count," said Lily, who had followed close behind.

Spread out over the portion of the lake fronting the construction site were twenty canoes, each with two Indians. In the canoe closest to shore stood Chetzemoka, the old Indian

Crescent Gold

from La Poel. He was naked except for a loin cloth, his long gray hair blowing in the wind, and around his neck, glistening in the morning sun, hung a gold pendant. He and the others were chanting in unison.

"Looks like a real big problem to me," said Rex, joining the crowd of onlookers.

"Lily," yelled Ed, "telephone that sheriff, Ben Maxwell."

"I already have. He's on the way, but it will be at least two or three hours."

"Okay ... damn ..." He turned to his lead man. "Get everyone to the office."

"What's that they're singing?" Rex said.

"No idea, some kind of Indian gobbledygook I suppose."

"Seems like my diving is off for a while, those buggers are right over the site."

Ed grumbled. "Not if I can help it. That sheriff better do something when he gets here or I'll use that Indian's necklace for target practice!"

By the time Sheriff Maxwell arrived the number of canoes facing Barnes Point had doubled. Ed was waiting for him at the dock and Maxwell could see by the glare on Ed's face that this was not going to be a good day. He was tired from the long trek from Port Angeles and frankly, he didn't know what he was going to do. He'd checked with the U S Marshall's office and unless the Indians were on private land, the Feds didn't think the Indians were breaking any laws. They might be obstructing construction, but who owned the water was up for grabs. His young son, Ben Jr., often told his father he wanted

Crescent Gold

to be a sheriff like his dad, but at times like this, Ben wasn't sure he'd wish the job on anyone. As soon as the ferry boat was even with the side of the dock, Ben jumped off. *Here goes*, he thought.

Ed Nelson was the first to speak and did so right in Ben's face. "It took you long enough. Christ, we've got a big ass mess here, and you're alone? No deputies? You'd better have some answers or …"

"Or what, listen Nelson, back off. I'm tired and as pissed as you are, so let's go see what's got your pants in a knot … what the hell was that?"

"Sounds like a gunshot to me," said Ed, acting as surprised as Ben. "Damn Indians are probably shooting at my guys."

Ben and Ed pushed through the circle of men to find Seamus O'Riley, one of the older men on the crew, lying on the ground, bleeding from a gunshot wound to his leg.

"The shot came from the lake," one of the men yelled, "stinking Indians, they're going to pay for this."

"Hold on, calm down," said Ben. He knelt beside Seamus who was being doctored to by Lily. She glanced up at Ed and then at Ben.

"It's not bad, sheriff, mostly a flesh wound," she said. "But I don't think Seamus here will be dancing any jigs on St. Patty's Day."

Seamus grinned. "As long as there's some good Irish whiskey, my dear, don't you count me out."

Crescent Gold

Ben chuckled, gave Seamus a pat on the head, then stood and confronted the man that had yelled. "You're sure the shot came from out there?" he said, pointing to the canoes.

"Damn toot'n, sheriff, right out there."

Ben left the men and walked to the shore. "Chetzemoka, one of you fire that shot?"

The old man who had sat down when the shot was heard, now stood again in the bow of the closest canoe. "It was not from any of my tribe. They are mistaken; the shot came from behind us." He pointed over his shoulder.

As Ben turned back toward the Wyle men, another shot ran out, and the bullet found its mark.

Crescent Gold

Forty-Nine

One by one the canoes disappeared as the sun set in the western sky behind Mt. Muller. In the food tent Seamus O'Riley lay on one cot, Sheriff Ben Maxwell on the other. Seamus' wound was superficial, the sheriff's injury more serious, as the bullet had torn through his shoulder. The path had missed any vital organs, but he'd lost a lot of blood.

Fortunately Ben remained conscious and had been able to stop the Wyle crew from getting rifles and firing at the Indians. Ed Nelson had been the most vocal about retaliating, but once Ben ordered him to stop, the others followed suit. Now, in the fading light, Ben slept, watched over by Lily who had been acting as nurse for both men.

Ed closed the tent flap and walked to the lake's edge where Rex Thornton stood smoking a cigarette.

"I thought we'd agreed to fire just the one shot," he asked Rex, who snuffed out his cigarette with the heel of his boot and quickly lit another, but did not answer.

"That way it would look like the Indians started it." Ed coughed. "How the hell can you smoke those damn things and still dive?" Again, no response. "Shit, Rex, are you going to answer me?"

Crescent Gold

"Smoking is my business, breaks the tension – as far as the second shot, I figured, why not – I had a clear shot at the sheriff, so I took it. Besides, these rubes think both shots came from the Indian canoes. With Maxwell out of the way, we can deal with those natives tomorrow and put an end to this mess and I can get back to diving.

"If they come back," Ed said.

"Oh, I think they'll be back, and a couple slugs in that old man should turn the tide, so to speak."

Lily felt Ben's forehead. "Your fever's gone. A good night's sleep and another days rest you should be ready to travel. You need to see a doctor. I've done all I can."

"Thanks, Lily. Listen, I want you to make a telephone call for me – right away."

As Rex had predicted the canoes started arriving at daybreak and Chetzemoka once again stood erect in the canoe nearest the water's edge.

The old Indian started yelling immediately. "Sheriff Maxwell, I wish to talk." When he didn't get any response, he kept repeating the request until Ed and several of the men walked to the rim of the lake.

"You bastards shot the sheriff," Ed shouted. "He's laid up, so I'll speak for him."

Chetzemoka didn't respond, only stood stoically in the canoe.

Crescent Gold

"Did you hear me you dumb Indian. I'm in charge here and unless you and your pals get out of here right now, we're going to give you some of what you gave us last night. I'll give you five minutes and then I'd better not see any of you shitheads within a hundred yards of here." When Ed finished speaking he raised his arm high above his head revealing the rifle he held in his hand. With his other hand he pulled out his pocketwatch. "The time starts now!"

"We did not fire the shots that hit your man and the sheriff," Chetzemoka yelled. "We only are protecting our sacred ground, and ..."

"Coming up on four minutes," was all Ed said.

Ed and the other men watched as Chetzemoka paddled to the closest canoe and talked to the young man in the bow.

"Three minutes," Ed yelled. He turned to one of the men. "Here, take my watch and when it hits five after, tell me." Ed inserted a 32 caliber bullet in the new Winchester, locked and took aim.

As the man turned to Ed to tell him two minutes to go, the canoes began paddling toward the other end of the lake, away from Barnes Point.

Ed decided they needed some incentive to paddle faster and fired off a round over the retreating Indians' heads. They didn't look back, but continued their slow, steady pace, all the while chanting the song from the day before.

"Think that's it?" Rex Thornton asked.

"I don't know, but for now we should be in the clear." He turned to the men. "Okay, it's back to work."

Crescent Gold

"Oh, oh, here comes trouble," Rex said, as he pointed over Ed's shoulder.

Ed turned to see Ben Maxwell, supported by Lily, limping toward them and the look on his face spoke volumes.

"What the hell do you think you're doing, shooting at those people? I told you not to shoot at them, you sick fool. You'll have the whole damned Indian nation down on us."

Ed shrugged his shoulders. "Looks like it got rid of them, no thanks to you."

Maxwell ignored the sarcasm, and with Lily's help walked within a foot of Ed. "Listen, that's it! Anymore shooting and I'll put you in handcuffs – got it!"

Nelson nodded, turned and walked away.

Fifty

A light breeze ruffled the lace curtain that hung over the open window in Sara Munn's Port Townsend hotel room. Sara and Jim sat on the edge of the bed. Behind them the eider down quilt was covered with sheets of stationery. "The air smells good, let's go for a morning stroll," Sara said, walking to the window.

"You mean we're done with the guest list and the dinner menu?" Jim asked, rising and joining her.

"Almost, be patient now Mr. Deputy U.S. Marshall, you promised." Sara pushed the curtain aside. "Hmm, smells good, I do believe Spring is finally on the way."

"That reminds me, Larry and his wife want us to come over tomorrow night for a St. Patrick's Day Party."

"I guess I could stay one more night," Sara said, walking to the room's open door. "C'mon, let's go for a walk, it's too nice a day to be cooped up in here."

Sara took one step out the door and collided with Larry. "Well, speak of the devil!"

Crescent Gold

"Oops, sorry Sara." He looked past her into the room. "Jim, telephone's been ringing off the hook. They've been trying to reach you since last night."

"Who, for crying out loud?"

"Some lady named Lily, from Crescent Lake."

"Guess I'll be taking that walk. Come with me," he said looking at Sara.

"All right, but I don't like the sound of this," Sara said, rising and following Jim and Larry.

Hello, Wyle Construction."

"This is Jim Albright, returning Lily's call."

"Sheriff, this is Lily. I was calling for Sheriff Maxwell, but he's better now and hold on, I'll get him for you."

"What do you mean, 'he's better now'?" Jim asked, but Lily was gone.

As Ed watched from shore, Rex disappeared beneath the surface. Ed figured they only had one more shot at it. Either the Indians would be back soon or the sheriff would interfere and delay things again. One thing he knew for sure, they didn't need an audience.

Ed looked past the spot where Rex had gone under and saw at least a half dozen of the canoes still pulled up on the opposite shore. He figured they'd seen Rex and it was only a matter of time before they returned.

The diving helmet broke the surface and Rex swam toward the shore. "I found a large box in a room at the back of the

Crescent Gold

building. Seems solid, but when I tried to lift it, I couldn't, too heavy."

"What did it look like?" Ed asked wading out a few feet to where Rex stood.

"Hard to see clearly in flare light, but I'd say it was about two-by-two foot, probably made of wood and, oh yeah, the top has what looks like a large bird either burned or etched into it."

"That's got to be it!" Ed said excitedly. "And you can't lift it. How about taking the top off?

"Maybe," he said, "but I need to get another air tank and some more flares. I'll try lifting it again, too. Maybe if I can get it out of the building, I can drag it in."

Five minutes later, Rex was back in the water.

"How's it going?"

Ed whirled around to see Lily walking his way.

"Ah … fine, Rex thinks he's found two good spots," Ed answered.

"Isn't he pretty far out? I didn't thing the dock was going to be so out from shore"

"No, not too far, he's got to look at all the possibilities."

Lily smiled. "Okay. Just so you know, Sheriff Maxwell is still plenty weak and shouldn't be up if his wound is going to heal, so he's asked the new deputy U.S. Marshall to come here in case there's more trouble with the Indians."

"What!"

"He asked me to call last night, but I didn't get through to him until this morning," Lily said. "I thought you'd be pleased to have the help."

Crescent Gold

"Why didn't you tell me about this last night?" Ed said, in a tone of voice that made Lily cower.

"I'm … er, sorry, I …?"

"Oh stop blubbering. Where's this deputy coming from?"

"From Port Townsend. Guess you didn't know, Jefferson County Sheriff Jim Albright is the new Deputy U.S. Marshall; he should be here this afternoon."

At that moment, Rex broke through the water, but seeing Lily, he didn't yell to Ed that he'd been able to lift the box out of the building and had begun dragging it to shore. He waved, trying to get Ed's attention.

Lily spotted him. "Oh look, there's Mr. Thornton."

Ed turned and waved to Rex. "Okay, Lily. Sorry I shouted. You go back now and wait for Deputy Albright, I really don't think we'll have any more problems with those Indians, but yes, it might be good insurance to have him around. Hurry on now, I've got to help our diver, looks like he's found a good spot for some pilings."

Fifty-One

As soon as Lily was out of earshot, Ed waded out and called to Rex. "I hope you got good news, because we don't have a lot of time."

"I've got the box about fifteen feet from shore. What's the problem?" Rex asked.

Ed waded out a bit farther and told Rex what Lily had just related.

"So your old enemy Albright is on the way here. Shit, just what we needed. Well, maybe he won't recognize you; you said you changed your appearance."

"Can't chance that, so we'd better get the box to shore and have a look-see before he gets here or the Indians come back."

"All right, here, take my helmet, I won't need it any more. I'll go back down and pull the box closer so you can help me bring it to shore," Rex said, disappearing once again under the water.

Ed carried the helmet to shore and then waded out until he was waist deep in the water.

A minute later Rex's head popped up a few feet away. He pointed down. "Reach down, you should feel it."

Crescent Gold

Feeling the box, Ed quickly glanced around before lifting it out of the water. "Let's carry it over behind that large hemlock; we should be out of sight there."

Rex nodded. "Okay, one, two, three and lift. Good, let's move."

"This has got to be it," Ed said, setting down his end of the box.

"How can you be so sure?"

"The heron on the top – the bird you saw, the heron is all over the map" Ed said, as he examined the top, trying to find how it was attached. "Geez, there's no hinge, how the hell is this thing on here?"

"Maybe they used some kind of nails," Rex offered, standing back and letting Ed examine the box lid. As he spoke, he looked back toward the lake. "No sign of the Indians."

"That doesn't mean they won't be back, but we don't care now. If I can just get this cover off, we can scram out of here. How about any of the crew, are they looking this way?"

"Nope. I saw your girlfriend and the mutt standing by the cabin, but that was a few minutes ago, while I was still in the water."

Ed stood up. "Well shit, I'm going to pry the damned top off with my knife."

Using his pocketknife, Ed pried up one corner, and then the next, fracturing the thin sides as he went. "That's it! Let's see what's in this baby."

Rex leaned over Ed as he lifted off the box lid.

"Well I'll be a son-of-a-bitch!"

"You got that right," said Rex.

Fifty-Two

Kaiahan grabbed S'Hai-ak's arm. "Be careful removing the top, the elders used small wooden pegs to hold it down and you may shatter the entire box if you pry up too hard. Here, let me help."

Slowly the two friends pried up the lid. "There," Kaiahan, said, "it is off."

S'Hai-ak reached in. "There are many pendants, no wonder we had trouble lifting."

"Yes, it is a treasure that took many moons to create at our summer home."

"What should we do now?" S'Hai-ak asked. "Carry these to our new home?"

As if in answer to the question, a bolt of lightning streaked across the western sky, next a loud thunder clap. Then a second strike lit up the sky, this time immediately followed by the thunderclap.

Kaiahan looked at the black clouds pushing their way. "Perhaps that is your answer."

"What do you mean?"

Crescent Gold

"I believe the great Storm God is unhappy. This box is sacred and we have disturbed its resting place."

"But the golden pendants, surely he knows these belong to our tribe," S'Hai̇-ak said, grasping several dozen and raising them to the sky, in the direction of the mountain..

Kaiahan looked toward the mountain where the Storm God dwelt. Another bolt of lightning illuminated the sky, appearing to originate from the top of the mountain. "Here is what I believe he wishes us to do."

S'Hai̇-ak listened and nodded his head in agreement.

Fifty-Three

Rex held the pendant in his outstretched arm. The fading sunlight reflected off its surface, making it appear as if the etched heron was taking flight.

"So this is what you were after?" he said, lowering his arm and holding the pendant within inches of Ed's face.

"I … there's got to be …ah …"

"One lousy, stinking gold trinket – that's it!"

"I don't understand," Ed said. "Something's wrong, there must be another box – you must have missed it."

"You said this one, the one with the bird had to be it, and you can dive in yourself and take a look, you asshole, all this for one piss-ant necklace."

"Settle down, Rex, I'm sorry, I …, oh shit here comes Lily."

Ed grabbed the pendant from Rex and quickly stuffed it in his pocket. "Lily … ah, look here what Rex found on the bottom of the lake," he said pointing to the box.

"Looks like an old box of rocks to me," she responded, "what's so fascinating about that?" She looked from one to the other, hunching her shoulders. "Anyway, I thought I'd let you know that the ferry just left shore and should be here pretty soon. Sheriff Maxwell figures Deputy Marshall Albright will be on board."

"All right Lily thanks. I'll be up in a few minutes."

"Yeah, right after he eats some crow," Rex said. "Or after he takes over diving!"

Lily again glanced from one to the other, shook her head and walked back to the cabin.

"Well that really helped," Ed said, "she'll wonder what the hell's going on."

"I thought you had Miss Sweet Cakes in the palm of your hand?" Rex said snidely.

"Up yours, asshole. Listen, either you dive back in there and look again or we'll call our deal quits right now. I've got bigger problems with Albright on the way"

"It's too late for that Ed. Take a look." He pointed over Ed's shoulder.

The canoes had formed a large circle, the center of which was over the spot where Rex had been diving.

"Oh crap," Ed said. "Now, what?"

"Your call, but I'd say it depends on whether you want to face the sheriff. As for yours truly, Wyle still needs a diver one way or the other, so I'm sticking around, at least for a while. I don't have any reason to be afraid of Albright." Rex hesitated. "I think we found all there was to find, and with the Indians putting up such a fuss, well …"

"Hey, you fired those shots and …"

"Only you know that Nelson, or whatever your name is – and you'd better shut up about that."

Crescent Gold

"Oh yeah," Ed said, "think you win either way, do you ..." He swung at Rex.

"Screw you, Nelson, I ...Damn!!"

Lily waved as the ferry came in sight of Barnes Point. Jim Albright waved back. *Well, here goes, my first job as a Deputy Marshall,* he thought.

"Lily," he yelled, "I hope I'm in time."

She offered her hand. "Just in time, as a matter of fact, the Indians have returned and I know our foreman's ready to do battle."

"That's Ed Nelson, isn't it, your foreman?"

"Yes, and he's out by the lake with our diver, Rex Thornton."

"Where's Ben? I'd like to see him first."

"He's resting in the cabin, but he wants you to get over to the job site." She paused. "Listen, I need more wrappings for the sheriff's wound so I'm going to go over to the Marymere. I'll catch up with you later," Lily said, turning and not waiting for Jim to answer.

"All right then," he called, "if you see Ben before I do, tell him I'm here and after I get things under control, I'll be there."

The men along the shoreline slowly parted as the sheriff approached. Through the widening gap Jim could clearly see Chetzemoka standing ramrod straight in the bow of his canoe. Jim walked to one of the two Negro men on the Wyle crew.

Crescent Gold

"Cecil isn't it?" he asked the black man who he knew from Port Angeles.

"Yeah, sheriff, nice to see you again, understand you're our new U. S. Marshal. Congratulations."

"Thanks, Cecil, it's Deputy Marshall, by the way. Where's your foreman, Ed Nelson?"

Cecil pointed to Jim's left. "He was over there with that diver fellow, Thornton. Haven't seen either of 'em in the last few minutes." He glanced out to the lake. "At least since they came back."

"What's the old Indian's name that's standing in the closest canoe, do you know?"

"Chet ... z ...kay ... ah ... hell I don't know for sure, they all sound and look 'bout the same." He chuckled. "Folks like me and Henry over there get accused of that all the time." Cecil chuckled again at his little joke.

Jim nodded and walked to the water's edge. "You there, standing in the canoe. My name is Jim Albright and I'm a U S Marshall. Sheriff Maxwell asked me to come and help."

Chetzemoka remained standing, stoically.

Instead of yelling again, Jim wadded out, waist deep and motioned with his arm. Chetzemoka seemed to understand for he sat down and paddled to Jim. The Indian spoke first.

"I am Chetzemoka. Your white teachers gave me the English name of William. Like many of my ancestors before me, I am the S'Klallam tribe historian and protector of our heritage. My father was a great chief whom you Whites called the 'Duke of York'."

Crescent Gold

"The 'Duke of York', can't say I've heard about him, but as for you, do I call you William or Chetzemoka?"

"Chetzemoka – a S'Klallam name shared by generations of tribal historians."

Jim moved next to the canoe and offered his hand. "Proud to meet you, now let's see if together we can work out a solution to this mess – and then later, I'd like to hear more about your father."

The sage old man nodded and took Jim's hand.

Fifty-Four

The flames flickered across their faces making it look as if they were wearing streaks of black soot. Kaiahan yawned and leaned back against a moss-covered fallen tree trunk, his eyes barely open. S'Hai-ak raised a pouch to his lips, took a drink of water, replaced the stopper and tossed the pouch to Kaiahan, hitting him on the leg.

"Take a drink and I will fill it for our trip tomorrow."

Kaiahan raised the pouch. "It is almost empty. You were thirsty," he said, throwing the pouch back to S'Hai-ak.

"No wonder, with the afternoon heat and the weight of the pendants. I am not the youth I was."

"Nor am I, but remember it was your idea to carry most of the pendants."

"Yes, and it was your idea to fill the box with rocks and return it to the longhouse. We used much of our strength for that task," S'Hai-ak said. "We should have left more than the one pendant – our load would have been less."

Crescent Gold

"We agreed that one pendant would be sufficient to appease the Storm God, and I believe returning the sacred box was necessary. Future generations may return and use it as we did."

S'Hai̇-ak stretched out his lean frame. "As you wish, it is done, and I am ready for sleep; we will need to rise early to be in Tse-whit-zen before nightfall."

Kaiahan rose and walked to his friend. "Here, let me fill the pouch, and tomorrow we will better share the load."

Fifty-Five

There was blood on Rex Thornton's hand. He wiped his left eyebrow again – more blood. *That bastard!* Slowly he got to his feet. *What's that?* He turned just in time to see Jim Albright wade in the lake after calling to Chetzemoka. Using his handkerchief he wiped his forehead once more, brushed off the dirt and went to join the group at the lake's edge, where Jim Albright was standing waist deep, next to the canoe with Chetzemoka.

"What happened to you?" a man named Henry asked, "and where's Nelson?"

Rex hesitated. *I must look bad for him to notice – damn.* "Ah … hit my head on a log when I was coming ashore."

"You should have Lily take a look at that. How about Nelson, he was with you last time I looked."

"Don't know, he left me when I came in …"

"He left you – with a cut on your head … c'mon he's an ornery guy, but not that bad," said Henry.

"I'd like to know where Nelson is too!"

Crescent Gold

Rex whirled around to face Jim Albright who had waded ashore.

Though momentarily caught off-guard, Rex regained his composure and offered his hand to Albright. "We've never met, I'm Rex Thornton."

"Sheri ... Jim Albright, Deputy U.S. Marshall, from Port Townsend. I've seen you around, you're the diver, right?"

"Yup, I'm the diver, but it looks like my diving is over for today." Rex pointed to the canoes.

"From the looks of that head wound, it wouldn't have mattered anyway," Albright said. "As far as the S'Klallam, I think we've reached a compromise. I'll need to talk to your foreman wherever he is, or George Wyle when he gets back."

The building nearest the large tent and adjacent to the cabin served as the Wyle crew's tool storage shed. It also was where Ed Nelson secreted a few personal items including his pistol, money, his Canadian papers and the map he'd taken from Clayborne.

A large crack in the shed door allowed Ed a clear view of the scene at the lake's edge. He saw Rex walk to the group and he saw Jim Albright wade ashore.

When Ed had been told about Albright's pending arrival he knew a choice had to be made, and the nasty confrontation with Thornton made the decision for him. He felt he couldn't chance an encounter with Albright.

After leaving Thornton prone on the ground he'd walked quickly to the shed, intending to gather his belongings and leave immediately. Curiosity, however, had delayed him and

Crescent Gold

now two of the Wyle crew were standing in the path to the shed, only a few feet away.

Nelson had always known this moment would arrive, but since discovering the location of the Indian village he'd hoped to be leaving with a handful of gold rather than the single pendant now stuffed in his pocket.

He did not want to underestimate Jim Albright again. As Sven Olsen, Nelson had escaped before, but only good planning and a bit of luck had kept him one step ahead of the wily sheriff and allowed him to flee undetected. The question was should he wait till nightfall or chance leaving now. It had also occurred to Nelson that Rex Thornton could rat on him as far as the pendants and the village were concerned, but other than his association with Clayborne, Thornton knew nothing of Nelson's illegal escapades and the murders at Tubal-Cain. Nelson's best guess was Thornton would shut up and hope to stay on the Wyle payroll.

He looked again through the door crack. *Crap! Albright's looking right at me – what the hell?*

Cecil, Henry, Rex and the other men said in unison, "What's the compromise?"

"I'll fill you in on the details later, but if you move the location of the proposed dock several hundred yards toward the Marymere Hotel the Indians will not interfere. Better yet, work out an agreement to use the Marymere pier."

Rex didn't say anything, but the others shook their heads. "Makes sense to me," Cecil said.

Crescent Gold

"Okay," Albright said, "now I need to talk to either Wyle or that illusive foreman of yours." He looked toward the cabin. "But first I'm going to see how Ben Maxwell is, and ... ah ... that's odd. Look at that dog."

Fifty-Six

Lucky stood on his hind legs and scratched on the shed door, all the time wagging his bushy tail.

"Scat, go away Lucky, shoo," Ed said in as forceful a voice as he could muster without shouting.

Lucky sat down and cocked his head, then gave two loud barks.

"Lucky, no barking. Go find Lily. Lucky, get Lily."

The Lab got up, but instead of obeying the voice he recognized as Ed's, started whining and with a quick leap, renewed his scratching at the door.

Ed was at a loss. No matter what he commanded, Lucky was undeterred.

He looked again through the crack. *Now everyone is looking at me. Damn!*

"I've got no choice now," Ed said out loud. He grabbed a few things and shoved the door open. "Here goes."

Whatever's in that shed, the dog wants it bad" Jim said.

"Probably a squirrel, crazy dog is always chasing them," said Cecil.

Crescent Gold

The words were hardly out of Cecil's mouth when the shed door flew open, knocking Lucky aside.

Rex was the first to react to what they saw. "Well, I'll be damned, the lost foreman is found!"

"Maybe he locked himself in," Cecil said. "Surprised he didn't yell in that strange language he uses when he's pissed."

Another crew member, Oscar Scheele, interjected, "ya I da only one who knows them is cuss words."

Jim, who'd been taking in the whole scene, turned to Oscar. "Why's that?"

"Cause I'm da only other Swede around here."

As Oscar said this, Ed emerged from the shed and the sun shone full on his face.

"Swede, you say," Jim said, and then something clicked in his memory and his thoughts raced – *that day at the mine when Sven Olsen cussed about the earthquake ... no, that's impossible. I've been thinking about, but ... The height's about right – with a beard ... a little older ... no, it can't be him ... son-of-a-bitch!*

"Hey, Nelson, hold on there!"

Nelson ignored Albright's call and disappeared behind the shed.

Albright turned to Cecil. "You keep a lookout for George Wyle, I'm going to see why Nelson went the other way, and Thornton, stick around. I've got some questions for you." That said, Jim took off at a trot toward the shed.

Ed quickly ran to the path which led to the road behind Wyle Construction Company's office and the Marymere Hotel, and

Crescent Gold

hurriedly made his way toward a secluded spot on the lake. Anticipating that he might sometime need a quick get-away Ed had secreted a rowboat under some overhanging tree branches where Barnes Creek flowed into the lake. His plan had been to row up the creek that flowed from Marymere Falls, ditch the boat and hike to Piedmont where he could hire a boat to take him across the Strait and back to Canada.

The weather had been unusual during March – very little rain on the north side of the Olympic Mountains. Barnes Creek was bone dry.

Nelson realized his options were limited. Quickly he decided to backtrack along the road to the hotel, pick up the Barnes Creek trail that led to Marymere Falls and eventually to the trail over Storm King Mountain.

He rounded the first turn in the road and ran into Lily. "Lily … ah …"

"Ed, what are you doing here?"

"Looking for you, c'mon let's go for a walk."

"Ed, I'm busy … got to get these bandages back to the tent."

At that exact time, Jim Albright broke through the brush lining the road. "Nelson!" he yelled, "Hold up there."

Ed ignored Albright's command, and grabbing Lily, headed up the road toward the trailhead.

Lily dropped the wrappings. "Ed, what's going on? You're hurting me!"

"Shut up and keep going."

Jim was in a quandary. He had no proof Ed Nelson had done anything wrong, and his mind still wouldn't let him believe

Crescent Gold

Nelson could be his old enemy Sven Olsen, but then, why was Nelson running away – what reason would he have for fleeing if he hadn't committed any crime? *Do I have any authority to stop him? Damn, it must be Sven.*

"Well, nothing ventured, nothing gained," Jim said aloud.

He quickened his pace and followed. "Ed, Ed Nelson, slow down, I need to talk to you." Nelson continued moving away and Jim could see that Lily was being forcibly pulled along. "Lily, you all right?"

Closing the gap, he again called out. "Lily!"

Lily and Ed disappeared into the woods.

Jim saw the sign that read, *Marymere Falls*. At the same moment he noticed for the first time he had a companion. Running next to him was the brown Lab, Lucky.

Fifty-Seven

The sun was low in the western sky when Kaiahan and S'Hai-ak sighted their village of Tse-whit-zen. It had been a grueling day of hiking and each man would be glad to unload his heavy sacks of pendants. S'Hai-ak had lost his footing on the ice during their steep descent from what the S'Klallam had dubbed "strong wind ridge." They had rested long enough to wash and wrap S'Hai-ak's bloodied arm, and eat an extra ration, thus making them trek the last three miles of the jagged and precipitous trail in the half-light of the afternoon.

"Only a short distance to go," Kaiahan said.

"Yes. You must be eager to see your mate and two children," said S'Hai-ak.

"I am – ah ... isn't it about time you found a mate?" He playfully poked his friend.

"Soon, very soon." He turned to Kaiahan. "I know I can't take any more journeys like this one – my strength is gone. I would not be able to pleasure a mate for several days." He laughed and poked back.

Kaiahan nodded and smiled.

Crescent Gold

"Look, Kaiahan, someone is running out to meet us," S'Hai-ak said. "It is your son."

The entire village had been told to attend the evening campfire the next day and O'Wota was hurriedly cleaning their bowls after a hastily prepared meal. The walk to the longhouse would only take a few minutes, but she did not want her family to be late. Working with When-an-Ismo slung over her back added to the difficulty of her task, but by now she was used to carrying her daughter in this manner. Kaiahan and Patkanim had left to get more firewood and water for the next day. When-an-Ismo cried and O'Wota pulled the blanket wrap around so the child was at her chest.

"We should go now," said Kaiahan entering their room.

"Your daughter is hungry."

"Feed her on the way. Patkanim, help your mother with the pot and bowls, it is time to go."

The senior elder, Lach-ka-nam, was the last to enter and took his position of honor between the other elders standing in a semi-circle facing the gathered tribe of the S'Klallam.

"We are here tonight to honor two of our tribe," Lach-ka-nam said, without preamble.

A hush fell over the tribe.

"Kaiahan and S'Hai-ak, step forward."

Lach-ka-nam continued. "These two men have risked their lives to return to us the pendants that were stored in our former village. It would have taken us many moons to replace these

Crescent Gold

golden symbols of our tribe which we use for trading and sacred ceremonies. S'Hai-ak, kneel down."

Lach-ka-nam took a leather pouch fom his outer garment and removed a pendant. "For all your help and courage." He hung the pendant over S'Hai-ak's head and addressed the crowd. "He has done us great service." Then Lach-ka-nam smiled. "Perhaps this great honor will make it easier for you to attract a mate."

The crowd murmured assent.

The wizened old man next looked at Kaiahan. "Kneel. This member of our tribe not only convinced us to attempt the recovery of the pendants, but participated in the tasks, leaving his mate twice to travel long distances. Additionally, Kaiahan has made a painting on the wall of our summer dwelling that tells of our journey and shows the way back to Tien-ah should future generations someday want to return."

He again reached into the pouch and removed a pendant. "This sacred pendant is to honor you and all of your line. You will now have a second name as will your son and all that come after him. That name is Chetzemoka, which means 'honored recorder of times past'."

Kaiahan rose and turned to his tribe. "I accept this honor and I believe the great Storm God will someday guide our ancestors back to Tien-ah."

Fifty-Eight

Marymere Falls originates where Falls Creek descends from a craggy ridge and then drops steeply ninety feet into a rocky grotto. Barnes Creek flows from the grotto, past a stand of spruce trees, through moss-covered rocks and over a sandy beach into the lake.

A short distance up the often slippery trail, two single log bridges connect the bottom and upper parts of the trail. Several caverns can be seen when the water flow is at its lowest. The entrance to the largest cavern is only a few feet from the top of the ridge. Past this cavern, the trail climbs even more steeply on its ascent to the summit of Storm King Mountain.

Jim entered the falls trail and caught sight of Ed and Lily. He yelled again, "Nelson, stop right now." Lucky barked and ran ahead of him up the increasingly steep grade.

Nelson abruptly stopped. He pointed a gun at Lily's head.

"What the hell are you doing?" Jim cried out.

Crescent Gold

"What I'm doing is telling you to back off or I'll put a bullet in her head."

Lily squirmed in Nelson's grasp. "Ed, my God, why ... I ..."

"Shut up you cow and do what I say," Ed said, pulling Lily along toward a log bridge.

When the trail leveled off Jim could see Nelson and Lily crossing a log bridge. They were halfway to the other side, single file with Lily in front. There was little doubt now that Nelson was guilty of something or he wouldn't be running. Forcing Lily to go with him and threatening to shoot her was crime enough. Beyond the end of the bridge the trail disappeared behind an outcropping. Jim had a thought – *worth a try.*

"If you stop now and let Lily go, I won't follow you," he yelled, hoping Ed would hear him over the noise of the cascading water.

When they reached the other side, Ed stopped and turned to face Jim. "Y ... funderare Mig galet." Ed realized he'd spoken Swedish. "I ..."

That voice! A shadow cast by the spruce trees fell across Ed's face, emphasizing his two day beard growth. *My God, it is* ... "So it is you, Sven."

Nelson laughed. "I kinda figured you would have guessed that by now Albright."

Lily twisted around. "Sven? Who's Sven?"

"Sven Olsen, at your service, my dear. Now shut up and let's go."

Crescent Gold

He looked across the bridge at Jim. "You just stay over there – or else!" With that, he tightened his hold on Lily and dashed into the trees.

Lily continued to struggle in Sven's grasp. "Ed or Sven, or whatever your name is, why are you doing this, you said you loved me?"

"Stop your whining and keep moving." As he said this, the second log bridge came into view. "Once we cross this bridge, we start to climb, so save your energy for that."

Crescent Gold

Marymere Falls

Fifty-Nine

Jim had been on the Falls Trail before, when Sara, Honiko, he and Jesse had taken a day's outing during the Christmas holiday the previous year. The foursome had hiked to the top of the ridge, eaten a picnic lunch on the ledge at a cave's entrance and then descended. He knew, however, that past the cave entrance, the grade of the trail rose sharply and switch-backed toward the summit of Storm King Mountain.

He couldn't imagine Sven climbing very fast with Lily in tow. Without her slowing him down, Sven could make a faster ascent and possibly escape, especially if he made it over the ridge. Jim knew Lily was in grave danger, and he needed to act before it was too late.

Jim crossed the first log bridge and quickened his pace, ignoring the slippery moss on the second bridge. Mist surrounded him as he started up the rocky trail next to the waterfall. A few minutes later, he realized that Lucky had disappeared into the thick brush alongside the trail.

Crescent Gold

There was no sign of Sven or Lily as he neared the top of the ridge and spotted the cave where the creek began its downward plunge.

Sven kept a firm grip on Lily's arm as he rounded the last bend in the trail and stepped across onto the cave's ledge, pulling her with him. He pushed her into the dark recess.

"Sit down in there and be quiet, I want to see if Albright is following us."

Sven looked over the edge. "Damn, the mist is too thick." He looked back at Lily who was squatting in the corner of the cave opening. "I told you to get in there!"

"It only goes a few feet," she said. "Ed, or whatever your name is, no matter what you've done, it can't be that bad."

"I've done plenty, including putting a bullet in the head of a loud mouth, smart ass woman like you, so if you know what's good for you, you'll clam up and do as I say. Albright knows who I am now, so knowing him, he'll not give up." He turned back to her. "Last time I got away, I got lucky – could have, as you American's say, 'checked out' in the deep blue sea."

He looked over the edge again. "Dammit, there he is!" He reached back into the cave, grabbed her arm and drug her to the edge of the ledge. "Albright! Guess you didn't understand." Sven pulled Lily to her feet, twisting her arm behind her back. "If you come any farther I won't need a bullet, I'll just give her a little push."

Lily squirmed. "Ouch – Ed that really hurts, and oh … not so close … oh my God, you wouldn't." she turned her head and the expression on his face told it all, he would!

Crescent Gold

"I told you to shut up," he said pushing her roughly down to her knees. Then he slapped her hard across the face. Lily screamed.

"Hear that, Albright." He looked over the edge, but this time Marymere Falls' mist obscured his view. "I can't see you now, but I know you're there, and the closer you get the rougher it'll be on Lily and then, whoosh, over she'll go. It'll be your fault." He yelled above the din of the rushing water.

Lily started sobbing and Sven took a step toward her. "This next one's just for you, Albright, just for you," he yelled hysterically, and raised his hand to strike her.

The excruciating pain shot through his body. It was as if someone had clamped his leg in a bear trap. Looking down he saw the wild eyes of his attacker, the animal's powerful jaws locked on his calf. He slammed down on Lucky's neck with the barrel of his gun, but the dog held firm. A scream welled up in his throat. He kicked at the dog's underbelly with his other foot, and missed. The pain increased. He dropped his gun.

He tried clamping his hand over the dog's upper jaw and pulling, but still the dog held firm and Sven's hand came away covered in his own blood. He sank to his knees and reached for the pistol. "Now, you mutt!"

He fired, but the shot just grazed Lucky's front leg. It was enough, however, as the Lab yelped and released his grip.

Sven rolled away from the dog, got to his knees and pointed the gun once more at Lucky's head. "This should do it!" The

Crescent Gold

gun didn't fire. "Damn it jammed!" Sven rose and stepped back ...

Jim had stopped cold when he heard Lily scream. When Sven yelled his next warning it sounded to Jim like some madman, a fanatical man, much like he remembered the villain's character behaving in a play he'd seen at the Rose Theater in Port Townsend. He was, as his father had often said, "between a rock and a hard spot."

The next scream he heard was a man's.

Sixty

Lucky growled at Jim as he approached, but didn't leave Lily's side.

"You all right?" he asked, keeping his distance. She didn't answer and he could barely make out her face in the dark recess of the cave. He could see the dog's bared white teeth, however.

"Lily, it's me, Jim Albright."

Then, faintly, "Yes I'm okay. Lucky's not though."

"Come on out, and I'll stay put, just in case the dog decides I'm a danger to you."

"What happened to Ed ... ah, Sven?" she asked, emerging from her hiding place with her hand around Lucky's neck.

"I don't think we'll have to worry about him anymore unless he suddenly sprouted wings."

Lily didn't seem to get Jim's meaning, but then she slowly nodded. "I was such a fool."

"Bring the dog over here." He squatted down and reached out his hand. "Come on Lucky, good boy." The dog limped to Jim and licked his outstretched hand. "Good dog."

Crescent Gold

Jim very carefully examined the dog's leg. "Not too bad." He took his knife out and cut off one of his sleeves. "This will have to do for now," he said wrapping the cloth around Lucky's leg.

"Think you and the dog can make it down?"

"Yes, and if I have to, I'll carry him – pretty well saved my life, I think."

Jim offered his hand to Lily. "Let's go then. I gotta warn you, it may not be a very pleasant scene down below."

The twisted, broken body of Sven Olsen lay face down in the middle of the pool and the water flowing out of the grotto was red with his blood.

"You and the dog stay here," Jim said as he left the trail and waded into the pool. Even though he knew Sven had to be dead, he felt for a pulse – none. He took hold of the dead man's collar and pulled the lifeless body out of the water.

Lucky left Lily's side, limped to the body, sniffed, growled softly and then slowly backed away.

Jim turned the body over and Lily gasped. "Oh my God.!"

"Lily, I'm going to leave him here for now, and walk you back to the office." As he rolled the body over something fell from Sven's pocket. It glistened.

"What's that?" Lilly said.

Jim reached down, picked up the pendant and held it up to sunlight. "This answers a lot of questions and I believe it's what brought Sven Olsen here."

Crescent Gold

After making sure Lily was okay and bringing Ben Maxwell up-to-speed, Jim went to look for Rex Thornton. Halfway to the lake shore he met George Wyle.

"Jim, good to see you again, I guess I missed all the excitement."

"You sure did. Listen, I'm looking for that diver, Rex Thornton."

"He's gone, but he gave me a message for you. He's on his way back to Port Townsend, say's if you want to see him, he'll be there, and he left these for you." He handed Jim several pieces of board. "I didn't quite understand the rest of what he said, something about gold pendants and the box they were hidden in under the water in the lake. He figured you'd know what to do with them." Jim looked at the boards and noticed the designs on several of them matched the symbol on the pendants they'd taken from Spencer Clayborne and the one he'd just found with Sven Olsen, alias Ed Nelson.

Jim smiled. "Yes, I think I can figure that out. C'mon, I need to fill you in on what I know and by the way, you'd better be looking for a new foreman. The old one's permanently out of commission."

And Jim added, "Finally!"

Crescent Gold

Gold!

Gold! Gold! Gold! Gold!

Bright and yellow, hard and cold

Molten, graven, hammered and rolled,

Heavy to get and light to hold,

Hoarded, bartered, bought and sold,

Stolen, borrowed, squandered, doled,

Spurned by young, but hung by old

To the verge of a church yard mold

Price of many a crime untold.

Gold! Gold! Gold! Gold!

Good or bad a thousand fold!

How widely it agencies vary,

To save - to ruin - to curse - to bless –

    From a poem by Thomas Hood

Epilogue

April 1908

A fire burned brightly in the fireplace in Chetzemoka's small cabin on Lake Crescent. Every chair was taken and if the people had been attending a play, there would have been a sign saying, "Standing Room Only."

Besides Chetzemoka and several members of the S'Klallam tribe, those present included: Jim Albright, Sara Munn, Ben Maxwell, Avery Singer, George Wyle and Lily Ellis.

Ben Maxwell stood with Chetzemoka in front of the brick fireplace.

"I asked Chetzemoka to invite you all here tonight so you could be brought up-to-date on plans for Singer's Lake Crescent Tavern and to witness a special presentation by Jim Albright," Maxwell said. "Avery Singer, you're on."

Singer detailed the agreement with Chetzemoka that gave the tavern owner the rights to build a new dock for his tavern, but several yards north of the original site. He went on to say

Crescent Gold

however, that he had worked out his own agreement with the Barnes's family to use the Marymere Hotel's dock until the road was completed. He thanked Chetzemoka and invited him and any of the S'Klallam to be guests at the grand opening the next year.

"Guess that's it. Jim, your turn," Avery Singer said.

Jim walked to the front and stood next to Chetzemoka.

"During the fracas last month, I was happy to help Ben, and once and for all, be able to close the chapter on the Tubal-Cain Mine murders. What many of you may not know is that Sven Olsen, who used the alias Ed Nelson, had a map that showed the location in Lake Crescent of an ancient S'Klallam village where he thought he would find a cache of gold pendants. His main incentive for hiring Rex Thornton was to have him dive into the sunken village and recover the pendants. Thornton found a box that at one time may have held the pendants, but only one pendant was in the box."

He motioned to Sara. "Sara, please hand me that package."

Jim took the parcel and turned to Chetzemoka. "Inside you will find all the pieces to the box, which I've been told is very sacred to your people. Also, the package contains the one pendant that was in the box." He paused. "I've been assured that should you want to return the box to the submerged longhouse, Wyle Construction will help in any manner possible."

Chetzemoka smiled and took the package. "For myself, all the S'Klallam and our forefathers, I thank you." He opened the package and setting aside the box parts, removed the pendant. "S'Klallam means 'Strong People' and we believe that you,

Crescent Gold

Jim Albright, are one of the strongest of men, so we want you to have this pendant as a symbol of our thanks – and, if you please, our wedding present to you and your bride."

"As for the box you recovered, we have been asked to submit an article of our culture for exhibit at the Alaska-Yukon-Pacific Exposition in Seattle next year. The elders are in agreement; this sacred box will be our contribution."

Jim shook Chetzemoka's hand and the two men acknowledged the crowds applause.

"There is just one more thing," Jim said, "I got a telephone call this morning from Jesse Grayson, whom many of you know is the reporter from San Francisco. He has finished his book about the murders in the Tubal-Cain mine and asked me to thank all of you for your contributions. It will be published next year. Guess that's it, thanks again."

Now's the time to take my shot – Albright's mingling with the crowd outside the Indian's cabin.

He had earlier mixed in with the overflow throng while the meeting was going on in Chetzemoka's house. The story of the sheriff's exploits and tonight's gathering had appeared in all the peninsula's newspapers, even Shelton's *Daily Journal*.

What amazed him most, Olsen was really dead, Clayborne and Monroe, too. That made him the last of the gang. He'd agonized over whether Albright would come after him now. Months had pasted. Would he recognize him? His fringe of dark red hair now peppered with gray, his frame padded by several pounds, a new name. Add to that a good job at the mill, a decent place to live and a budding romance, Frank had changed profusely, inside and out – life was good. But, that would end if ...

Albright was moving away, climbing into a carriage. Frank reached under his coat, felt the handle of the Browning. As he pulled out the pistol, Albright stood in the carriage and waved to the crowd. *A clear shot ... now ... I ...*

Frank Jones released his grip, turned and faded into the Lake Crescent night.

Historical Background and Acknowledgements

The Log Cabin Hotel was the first hotel built on the shores of twelve-mile-long Lake Crescent. The hotel was built in 1895. It burned down in 1932.

The Marymere Hotel on Lake Crescent's Barnes Point, was opened in 1906. It was the first hotel built on the lake's south shore. Advertisements claimed it was, "The most centrally located resort on Lake Crescent." That the hotel offered, "the most natural attractions, most groves and beautiful trails."

The Marymere Hotel burned down in 1914.

Singer's Lake Crescent Tavern was built between 1914 and 1916. Over the years the ownership changed several times, additions were made and the tavern was eventually named Lake Crescent Lodge, its name today. The lodge was sold to the National Park Service in 1951.

Crescent Gold

There are countless stories about finding gold on the Olympic Peninsula, a few factual, most fictional.

Following the first documented exploration into the interior, during the summer of 1885, there were hundreds of forays by prospectors convinced that gold was "in them thar hills." A fun read is W. C. Jameson's *Buried Treasures of the Pacific Northwest*. One chapter chronicles the discovery of gold nuggets on a ridge near the Brothers Peaks in what is now Olympic National Park.

Even as early as 1877, gold nuggets were found along the North Fork of the Skokomish River in Mason County.

There were several significant mining claims filed in the Lake Crescent area, but these were primarily for manganese and copper. The majority of the successful gold mining operations were conducted along the Pacific Coast from Cape Flattery to Grays Harbor. Perhaps the most successful were in the early 1920's at Shi Shi Beach and near the mouth of the Ozette River.

The site of the S'Klallam Indian village of Tse-whit-zen was unearthed in Washington State's Port Angeles harbor in August 2003. Evidence indicates the site had been occupied for over 2500 years. It is the largest Indian village ever found in the Puget Sound region.

There is no evidence of a sunken S'Klallam village in Lake Crescent. The S'Klallam, on the other hand, did inhabit a region of the Elwha River and the lake. In the story, Chetzemoka and the S'Klallam canoe across Lake Crescent,

Crescent Gold

however, legend says the S'Klallam never canoed across as they feared "icy fingers would pull you under, and hold you in the bottomless depth."

Special thanks to my wife Jeanette for her inputs and especially for another outstanding cover design.

During the time I was writing *Crescent Gold*, I joined a new writer's group that meets at the Hoodsport Washington library. As with prior novels, the inputs I received from this group were very helpful.

Lastly, very special thanks go to Linda Steffen, my diligent editor. This is the third book she had edited for me and what an asset she is to my writing. Publication would not have occurred without her thoughtful and thorough efforts.

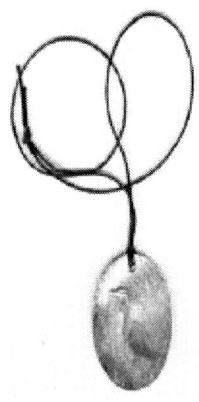